WALKING AMONG BIRDS

WALKING AMONG BIRDS

MATTHEW HICKSON

Magdalen College Press

This book is a work of fiction. The names, characters and events in this book are the products of the author's imagination or are used fictitiously. Any similarity to real persons living or dead is coincidental and not intended by the author.

Walking Among Birds

Published by Magdalen College Press

ISBN (paperback): 9781642376555
eISBN: 9781642376548

Library of Congress Control Number: 2019943231

CHAPTER I

"Whenever you feel like criticizing anyone…
just remember that all the people in this world
haven't had the advantages that you've had."

—*F. Scott Fitzgerald, The Great Gatsby*

I f I could run and never grow tired, then I think that I would like to run a lot. In fact, perhaps I would love it so much that I would run everywhere I went. As for me, at the moment, the most strenuous exercise I do is my many laps to the fridge and back, and the only chance of seeing me running is at the mention of "free donuts." Like many people, I have great intention to live what I idealise as a "successful life"—you know, those people that wake up at five am every morning, go for a run, drink lemon-infused water, send emails. I once knew a person like that, he was the kindest, smartest, most tenacious person you'd ever meet. He could sort out his life by six in the morning and then go about his day solving all the world's problems, one small act of kindness at a time. I hold dear to my heart every intention of being, crudely put, *that sort* of person.

But intention is not reality, and unfortunately intending to do something, anything, makes zero difference unless acted upon. I'm sure you've all heard that hilarious joke about the minister that moves to a small country town and encounters a friendly ghost in his rectory that he tries to prove exists by taking a photo—you know, the one with the punchline "well the spirit was willing but the *flash* was weak." Perhaps that joke and the saying it originates from is more about the need to prove our intentions than anything else. I sometimes think that the saying these days should be "the spirit is weak and the flesh is weak," for really our flesh's weakness should be no match for our spirit's perseverance. Anybody, myself included, can harp on about how the world is a broken place and is in desperate need of heroes, or even useful members of society—those allusive "fellows" who build up the community and act with integrity. But without action all those words are futile. It is often the case that those who complain the most about a problem do the least to change it.

I have a trick in the morning—a habit if you will that I do without fail. I always set my alarm for five o'clock—and when I wake up at that time each morning, a thought flashes through my mind as quickly as a blink of an eye: "Today could be the day I get up early, today could be the first day of the rest of my life." I pause on it for about five seconds, whereby I flail an arm in the general direction of my alarm clock and switch it off. I roll over while simultaneously pulling the covers up, and comfortably go back to sleep. Perhaps comfort is our worst enemy because it is the most hidden of all our enemies. The mantra of "due tomorrow, do tomorrow" is a dangerous one: idle hands are the Devil's workshop.

To that end, we come inevitably as we must to the story. Fortunately, this book isn't just filled with my witty puns and thoughtful discourse—though if you'd like more of that, please do get in contact with me. It hasn't been an easy task, but I have taken it upon myself over the last number of months to diligently try and collect all the relevant evidence and information so that I can retell accurately the events that you are about to read.

Our story is about a boy named Jack Lapin, although it's not really *about* him as such, but our story does *begin* with him. Jack had acquired exactly the same habit as myself. Every morning he awoke at five a.m. and went for a run...or at least, he meant to. I wish I could say that he jumped out of bed and gaily greeted the rising sun with his head held high and his hands on his hips, that he inhaled fresh blades of air through his nostrils as if to say "come get me, world" with a twinkle in his eye and a cheeky grin on his face. But I would be lying. Though, on the other hand, he wasn't particularly lazy for boys his age—you'll see that if you take a cross-section of sixteen-year-old males, most of them (surprisingly) don't get out of bed that early. He was just an ordinary boy—shorter than shoulder-length brown hair with a swept-over look at the front, intense bright, blue eyes against a backdrop tinged with bronze, and a warm smile that could convince anybody that there was nothing wrong with the world. All in all, a handsome but lanky young man.

On this particular morning, he was woken up by his brother eating breakfast downstairs, clinking the spoon on the side of the cereal bowl every time he scooped up a coco-loop from the surrounding milk. Of course, this sound wouldn't be annoying if the spoon was in the hand of anybody else, but to Jack, the most inconvenient truth in the entirety of human existence was his brother—especially when Jack's wiry, lean frame was sprawled over his bed sweating after a long hot night without much sleep, lying on his stomach with one leg dangling over one side of the bed, the other leg over the opposite side. They say absence makes the heart grow stronger—well, these two had been together their whole lives. They shared a womb, shared a childhood, and now were forced (oh, the humanity) to share an adolescence.

"Peter!" he yelled, cupping his hands like a megaphone.

No response.
"Peter! Eat quieter."
No response.
"Oi Peter! Shut up!"
Still no response, and so plan B kicked in.
"Daaaaaadddddd!"
And yet another deafening silence.

Jack quickly weighed up the options in his mind—stay in bed and suffer the "tink, tink" in the distance, or get up and cause a stir. You know what they say, a spoon in the hand is worth two in the bowl. He decided on the latter, pulling himself out of his sweaty Elysium of comfort and marching towards the stairs scantily clad in just his pyjama bottoms, making sure he muttered the whole way down to show his indignation, thinking where he could tell Peter to shove the spoon. He stormed into the kitchen and much to Peter's surprise, he grabbed the spoon out of his hand and threw it on the floor.

"Hey, I was using that to…"

"I don't care. You damn well know that you're being annoying, so stop it."

At this, Peter stood, ready to square-up and confront his twin.

"Well, at least I'm not going to be late. We're being picked up in ten minutes and you're still not dressed. So, I guess I actually did you a service by waking you up, twit."

With that, he gave Jack a little push in the chest—a move which was sure to start a scuffle if their father hadn't walked in at the exact same moment, whereby causing Jack to fall backwards in a theatrical stunt of choreographically crafted genius.

"Dad, did you see that? He pushed me into the cupboard," Jack said, grabbing his arm as if to imply he'd gotten a fatal wound on the way down.

Their father took his eyes off his paper and peered from over the top of his glasses.

"Peter, that's not very nice is it. And Jack, why aren't you ready? It's nearly time to go. Hurry along now, both of you."

Jack poked his tongue out into the "so there" face and Peter just stared at him with the usual brotherly malice. Jack had always been the scamp of the two, and the victim.

At his juncture, I feel it's important to tell you some of the history of the Lapin family, otherwise this scene we've just experienced might not make much sense. The twins' father, Roger, was born into a large litter of twelve children who together all lived in a sizeable yet humble middle-class house. He had gone to university to become an economist, a place where he met a beautiful woman by the name of Beatrice. The rest, of course, "is history" so to speak. They flirted, dated, and ended up being married (with all of Roger's large colony of a family in attendance). As economists, they dreamed of saving their money and eventually buying a mansion with a multitude of rooms and a warren of passageways. They endeavoured to be economically enriched.

But instead of monetary glory, Beatrice became pregnant and they got the two-for-one offer, giving birth to Peter at 12:36 am on a dark night in July, and to Jack eight minutes later. Of course, this made Peter admirable to the fact that he was older and therefore, logically, wiser. A fact that he had no gripes reminding Jack about whenever he needed to. As if having children wasn't enough of a tragedy for one lifetime, Roger then lost his wife when the boys were only two years old. There came a time when the boys had asked Roger why they didn't have a mother, and Roger had had to sit them down after school one day and explain the horrendous story of how she had perished in a gas-bottle explosion while filling her car up with fuel on the way home from work one day, never returning home and never being able to say a final goodbye to Roger or the boys. Whether she had been using her phone at the fuel pump, we will never know. In Roger's eyes, she was blameless.

And so the boys had no memory of their mother—for them, "dad" was always the word for food or a band-aid or some rare ounce of sympathy. Their dad worked the normal nine to five and apart from not having a mother, their life progressed relatively uneventfully. They went to an alright primary school in an alright neighbourhood. They had a couple of close friends each and many more friends on the periphery of their lives. When they were still little, Roger would come home every Friday evening after work and throw one of them over his shoulders while they giggled their little heads off. The weekends would be whiled away flying kites, or going ice-skating or bowling, or any other number of fun and meaningful experiences. In other words, they were as thick as thieves and content in their happy, small, "alright" life together. The three were, in a way, a triumvirate—perfectly content with each other's company but perhaps missing a fourth. They were like *Les Trois Mousquetaires*: Athos, Porthos, and Aramis, but where was d'Artagnan?

I wish I could say that was the end of the story and that you could have two little rosy-cheeked cherubs dancing around in your head forever, frivolously laughing away their summers, but alas, that cannot be the case. No story worth telling is ever purely about happiness. Primary school ended and with it they moved up to secondary school, and the cocktail of emotions and hormones that come with it. As with most people that age, everything became a competition. Their dad was no longer "cool," and friendships became more complicated, especially with girls. The bliss of weekends playing in the autumn leaves changed to a "go away, Dad," and the endless summers of punting along the river became "I'm busy," to the point where Roger gave up. He would trudge home from work Friday evenings and plonk himself down on the couch for a long night of TV and snacking whilst his sons did who knows what at who knows where with who knows…who?

It wasn't long until they got into trouble at school and were expelled for starting a fight between themselves and a group of other boys—a battle which even to this day Jack will claim they won, no matter what anybody else says. They went through a few schools, always being told to leave for one reason or another. Weeks of these deteriorating father-son relationships turned into months and months into a couple of years, until Roger had had enough. All of the stress led to him having a—to delicately put it—"large frame" (especially when standing next to his lean sons), and an odd twitch in the upper right-hand corner of his top lip. When he became agitated, the bristles of his small grey moustache would tremble in the air coming from his nostrils. Roger was the sort of man who always seemed to believe that some catastrophic occurrence was quivering unseen just over the horizon. His nervous disposition had not rubbed off on the twins. In fact, perhaps the opposite had happened. Many years of "get away from the pool—what if you fall in and drown?!" and "don't play wrestle near the windows in case you go crashing through one of them," had caused a sort of apathy to safety in their minds. In other words, they thought themselves bulletproof. But he worried more and more as the days went on. Because he loved them, it made it all the more difficult to tell them of his anxieties. He had made his decision last summer that they should be sent to the boarding school where his sister-in-law's twice removed cousin's brother's second cousin's aunt was the headmistress, and it is on the first day of their new school life that we have found them arguing over breakfast.

Deep down they were good kids, they just attracted trouble. As we grow, we come to learn that there are two intentions to our misdeeds: there is malicious bad behaviour, and there is jovial bad behaviour. We generally begin our lives practicing only the jovial bad behaviour, and by middle age, the malicious penchant within us bubbles up. As we grow old—for some of us—the jovial intentions often make a comeback. There is malicious bad behaviour, and there is jovial bad behaviour, and the twins were almost exclusively the latter. They may not have been conventionally labelled as "well behaved," but at least they *intended* to be "good kids." Just as Jack had every intention of being ready in time to be picked up – but, nonetheless, the doorbell rang and he was nowhere near ready.

Peter was first to the door, looking very dapper in his new school uniform: a white button up short-sleeved shirt tucked into grey shorts with long grey socks to match and freshly polished black shoes. The school crest sat on his breast pocket—a green shield surrounded by some foliage and the words printed almost microscopically on a banner: "Etiam capillus unus habet umbram," which, for the less Latin-inclined among us, roughly translates to "Even One Hair Casts a Shadow."

He opened the door and in front of him stood a sombre looking man with a long face and a black jacket.

"Good morning, sir," said Peter, giving a little smile and nod.

"Good morning, good morning. My name is Mr. Swinburne and I'm your chaperone to St. Benedict's today. Our driver's name is Mr. Algernon," he waved vaguely towards the car whilst opening up a piece of paper. "Do I have the pleasure of addressing Peter, or Jack?"

"Peter, sir."

"Very well, and where is your accomplice?"

"One second," Peter replied, holding up his index finger and then running off to find his brother.

"I'm so sorry, they're not ready on time, Mr. Swinburne. I assure you it won't happen again," Roger squeaked.

"Quite alright, Mr Lapin, quite alright."

And thusly they set forth on their journey, unknowingly on their way to events that would change their lives forever.

CHAPTER II

"The caterpillar does all the work, but the butterfly gets all the publicity."

—*George Carlin*

I always find it funny how people say that long trips are "all about the journey and not the destination." Well, when you think about it, they're often not, unless you intend on taking a trip without going anywhere. But I'm not sure many people do just get in a car, drive for a few hours without stopping and then complete the roundtrip home. If I really wanted to spend time with the people in that car, then I could've invited them all over to my place to have a meal and we could've saved some petrol money. Just like in life, if we focus on the journey and not the destination, then we are already setting ourselves up for failure. When we set a goal, we think, "but what if I don't succeed," and of course the next step is to justify our failure with "oh well, it's all about the journey and not the destination." If we focus on the journey, we may never reach the destination. Or perhaps it will only seem as though we'll never reach the destination.

This was the case for Jack and Peter as they stared out longingly at the passing flora and fauna: an endless array of bark, leaves, and birds beckoning to bored travellers to come and have a look, to change their destination. It seemed that they would never reach St. Benedict's College. Mr. Swinburne and Mr. Algernon had been discussing poetry the whole way with the usual interjections of those well versed in poetry such as "oh, I say," and "yes, I quite agree" when Peter decided to interrupt mid-sentence.

"Oh, yes, Charles, I much prefer it out here, where the world is qui…"

"Excuse me, Mr. Swinburne? May I ask what St. Benedict's is like? What should we expect?" Mr Swinburne was quite taken aback by this interruption to his grand and unnecessary explanation of the countryside, but thought for a second and then decided to humour his request.

"Well, expect the worst and you may be mildly surprised, Peter. As soon as we get there you have a meeting with the headmistress and she will welcome you and then get someone to explain the details and intricacies of school life to you."

"Head*mistress*?" Jack sneered.

"Yes, Jack, it's the word for a female headmaster," Peter said.

"Thank you, kind spirit. You're such an oracle of wisdom. Oh, thank you enlightened one. You twit, I know what a headmistress is...but don't you think it's strange to have a woman running a boys' school?"

They heard their father's voice in their heads— "Now now, boys, play nice." The night before, they had promised their father that they were to change their ways. In earnest, they had made that promise, and in solidarity they intended on keeping it. Again, the word *intended* rears its ugly head—for the thoughts of young men, or at least the terms in which they express them, are often marred with obvious suppression and disillusionment. As for Jack's confusion, there are a couple of obvious answers. The first is, of course, that there is no reason why a woman couldn't or wouldn't be running an all-boys school. The second is that St. Benedict's College had a sister school, St. Scholastica, and the headmistress was in charge of both schools together, overseeing the general running of both of them whilst delegating much responsibility to a deputy Headmaster for the boys' school.

As they approached the school, a pair of towers and a spire came into view and they passed by a large Victorian style façade of a building. Girls meandering about the gardens in their green and white checked dresses could be seen on the grounds in front of the imposing twin towers. Metal lettering on the gate spelt out the girls' motto: "Contendunt Vivere Obtulit Immaculatum" which is, of course, "Strive to Live an Unblemished Life." The building was fully encircled (apart from a couple of gates) by an old red brick wall, on which the other side sat St. Benedict's College, a square fortress of a building constructed in the Byzantine style. To the gulls flying high above these colleges, the differences between them would have seemed like mere nuances (for one, birds are not often experts on different architectural styles), but to those more wingless folk the contrast was stark. It was even embodied in their mottos: the male counterpart being of shadows, the female motto of a life lived in perfection. At least it was better than previously: it had only been a few years since the boys' motto had been changed from "Memento Mori," or "Remember, You Shall Die."

The girls' college, St. Scholastica's, was the original structure, with the boys' being built a few years later. It had been well looked after and year after year ranked among the top schools in the country:

an institution that prided itself on fine behaviour, strongly-held morals, and an unsurpassed level of well-rounded education. The gardens, adorned with their bright and happy arrays of flowers stretched out from the college building in all directions like rippling fields of golden wheat. The stems of lilies and lavender danced as the soft breeze swayed them this way and that like ballet dances coupling up for a euphoric *pas de deux*. The girls wandered happily along the winding garden paths discussing mathematical ideas, debating their own pensively deduced political viewpoints, and generally spending their break times doing whatever young soon-to-be successful women did.

Across the wall, or "the Great Divide" as the boys called it, was St. Benedict's. One only had to look over the partition to realise that occasionally "the grass is always greener on the other side" is true. There were only a few trees and grass spotted with patches of dirt here and there. The awards lauded to St. Benedict's were few and far between—it had become an unworthy, and sometimes unwanted shadow of its sister school. The boys were not allowed out for break unless doing a strictly supervised activity, so when the Lapin's car processed through the iron gate, they were welcomed by an eerily quiet ghost terrain. The only movements were the branches swaying gently but austerely in the same breeze that caused such beauty on the aforementioned "brighter side" of the wall. All would have been peaceful except that at that very moment, Jack thought he saw something quite a distance away, but moving closer at a rapid pace.

"What is that there, on the left there, sir?"

"That's a tree, Jack," Peter butted in.

"I wasn't asking about that, you…" Jack began to reply, but just as he was about to select a choice word for his brother, Mr. Swinburne slammed on the brakes with a mighty screech, as two boys ran in front of the car: a small bare-chested blond lad, and in hot pursuit of him a larger brown-haired boy holding what would appear to be the first boys shirt.

"What the flip do you think you're doing?" roared Mr. Swinburne from the passenger side. "Get in the car this instance, both of you!"

The taller boy thought for a split second and then, speaking with a very slight Francophone accent answered, "Sorry for making you stop like that, sir. Thomas was on his morning run, his *course du matin*, and he forgotten to wear his shirt, so I was chasing after him with it. He has very pale skin, sir, and I don't want to see him have the sunburnt. The sun, it is very bright today."

The younger boy, apparently Thomas, just stood there with his eyes cast down in embarrassment.

"Now really, Lorenz, of all the ridiculous…"

"Please, sir, it's true. I swear, look at him, he's like a duck out of water in this sun…"

"Get in the car, now!" Mr. Swinburne roared.

And so the two boys obliged, squeezing into the back seat with Peter and Jack, a room only meant for three people.

Jack gave a meek and awkward smile to the both of them as they squeezed in together. Lorenz smiled back whilst Thomas just looked down at his feet and wished with all his heart to not be in that car with his pursuer and two complete strangers.

"You know, I'm quite sure it's '*fish* out of water,' not '*duck* out of water,'" Peter told Lorenz with a small smile. Peter looked at his watch—the face had cracked when the car stopped suddenly and Peter's wrist had hit the seat in front of him.

The remaining thirty seconds of the drive up to the front of the building was done in absolute silence. After which they disembarked the car and entered through the arched door into a reception area, and at once all four were ushered in by Mr. Swinburne to the deputy headmaster's office and greeted by a warm-looking, well-built man standing up from his office chair to enthusiastically shake their hands.

"Ah, good morning, good morning. You must be Peter and Jack. My name is Mr. Latan…Charles Latan. I'm the deputy headmaster. Unfortunately, 'the boss' is very busy at St. Scholastica's and so it is not viable for her to come meet you today—my sincerest apologies, boys. Now, Mr. Swinburne. To what reason do I owe the delight of the company of Master du Sabre and Steerforth on this fine morning?"

"Good morning, Mr. Latan. I nearly ran them over on my way up the drive. They were running around creating all sorts of trouble, they were extremely fortunate not to get hit."

"Ah, I see. Thank you, Mr. Swinburne," at which point the chauffeur left the room and the boys were left with the smiling man. "Excuse me, boys," he smiled to Peter and Jack. "So, Lorenz. What happened?"

"Well, sir, as I explained to Mr. Swinburne, I was just enforcing the school rules, as Thomas run outside to get out of doing his morning chores and I thought I better follow to be remind him of…"

"It's not true" the younger boy said in a soft, delicate voice—the first thing the twins had heard him say so far. Lorenz at once shot him a glare and continued.

"Chores are very important, sir. The château cannot stand without the proper housework and…"

"I say, why aren't you wearing a shirt, Tom?" Mr. Latan interrupted, as if ignoring Lorenz and coming to a sudden realisation that the boy was shirtless.

Tom once again answered while staring down at his shoelaces. "He wanted my morning tea and jumped me. He grabbed my shirt and it slipped over my head…" The boy was almost down to a whisper by the end of the sentence, trailing off into the oblivion of silence.as everyone leaned in to try and catch what he was saying.

"I see. Is this true, Lorenz?"

"Well, technically, yes, sir. This is what has happened. But he is at the same fault as what I am. If he had given me his morning tea, I wouldn't have had to chase him. And it is an unsaid rule that lower grade students follow the orders of us more senior students, is it not?"

The man seemed to by mulling all this over in his head.

"And then, to run outside when it's strictly prohibited to be the outside at that time. Well, really all I did was follow him. I am not to blame for us being outside, that is his fault."

Mr. Latan's face twisted in deep thought, seeming to become more agreeable.

"And then, well, I barely touched him so for his shirt to come off with so little force it surely must not have been tucked in to start with, let alone the fact that not wearing a shirt is a very serious uniform violation. And the car…again, if he hadn't been running, I wouldn't have been chasing him. He was the instigator in each way. *Je n'suis pas responsable.*"

Mr. Latan continued to look as if he had a complicated mathematical equation going 'round and 'round in his head. After a few moments, he finally came up with a solution.

"Well, I guess all that is technically true. Lorenz, you may go, though may I say that he is a boy and you are a young man. I expect better from a man of your heritage and upbringing. And as for you, Thomas, you are in breach of numerous school rules, so I will see you at lunch time today and tomorrow for detention, and you will need to do Lorenz's chores for the next week for the trouble you've caused him. And did I see chocolate cake was for morning tea? I'm afraid I will have to confiscate that…as evidence. Next time, just give him the cake and avoid all this trouble. Go and wait outside the door there."

Peter and Jack remained sitting in their chairs gobsmacked at the whole ordeal—they glanced at each other at the same time both with an expression of "what just happened?" The phrase "I wouldn't have been chasing him if he hadn't been running" being a reason for acquittal seemed ridiculous. Technically true, but ridiculous nonetheless.

"Now, you two. Welcome to St. Benedict's. Sorry you had to experience that ordeal in your first ten minutes here. Some kids like Tom never learn their place. You have the rest of today to orientate yourself around the school. As you've been told, we have a peer-support program at the school and so you two will be looking after a group of younger students from varying years. After lunch, they will give you a tour of the school and you can get to know them. For now, you may go to your dormitories to unpack and get settled. Thomas is waiting outside and will show you both to your rooms."

He wrote the two room numbers on a slip and handed it to Thomas who then took both their bags and started walking towards the set of stairs on the opposite side of the reception room.

"Oh, no, that's quite alright...Tom, is it? I can carry my bag, and Jack can carry his," Peter offered.

A voice came sternly from the now distant deputy headmaster's office. "No, that's quite alright. Thomas can carry them."

"Okay . . . sorry," Peter said with a shrug to Tom.

They slowly trudged up two wooden flights of stairs, following little Thomas greatly struggling with the bags that were almost as heavy as him, dragging them up one stair at a time with great labour. Feeling guilty with every wince of the young boy's face.

"You know, Tom, I don't blame you at all for what happened between you and Lorenz. I...*we*...both think that was Lorenz's fault." If Peter couldn't offer a physical crutch, perhaps he could offer an emotional one. Thomas just stayed quiet and didn't make eye contact, as if Peter had said nothing at all. They went down a few winding passageways, passing interested looking boys the whole while, finally reaching Peter's room first, and Jack's room a few metres down the hallway. Jack thanked Tom and gave him a pat on the back, to which he got no reply or acknowledgement. He was left standing at his door as he watched Tom continue to wander down the hallway to wherever it was he had his next engagement.

All the other boys were about to head to class so Peter and Jack spent the next hour or so unpacking and settling in alone, and finding necessities such as the nearest toilets, showers, and other things. Both boys were "bunking" with another boy that they would be able to meet at lunch time. During their time alone, they continued wondering why Tom had been treated so unfairly.

This is where I can chip in with a bit of back-ground information. You see, it's often the things that are not said which have more of an influence than those that are. Mr. Charles Latan always had in mind, but never discussed, the circumstances by which both those boys had found their way to his school. Lorenz du Sabre was the son of the famous French General,

Lance du Sabre–a highly decorated military figure from Lyon with many years of experience and qualifications under his belt. Lorenz had a sister, Charmaine, who studied at the school next door. The du Sabre family was quite wealthy and had often donated large sums of money when called upon to help the school, and the prestige of having a decorated General's children (even if it was a foreign General) was welcomed by both schools.

Charmaine du Sabre was a fascinating young lady. She was the sort of sixteen-year-old that all the other girls aspired to be, and that all the boys her age aspired to be with. She was beautiful, but not in a submissive doe-like way. She had her father's chiselled jaw line and well defined features, a trait she shared with her younger brother. She had dark sandy-blonde hair and striking green eyes with which she could argue anybody down, boy or girl who dared defy her, and manipulate almost anybody into seeing her version of things. Lorenz was slowly becoming more and more like her, following in the footsteps of her manipulative and harsh ways.

She was currently in a "relationship" (at least, as much of a relationship as a large wall down the middle would accommodate) with a student at St. Benedict's—a fact that benefitted her brother to no end. You see, Lorenz was under a sort of unofficial "protection" from the boys in the upper echelon of the school. Any boy that didn't look upon Lorenz with at least the smallest bit of *fratenité* was not welcome in the hallowed group of senior students headed by the cock of the school, Cole Black. As you can guess, Cole was Charmaine's boyfriend (of course, the most beautiful girl will instinctively choose the most popular stag). And so Charmaine controlled Cole on a tight leash, and Cole controlled most of the boys in the upper form, providing Lorenz with a very comfortable position from which to become a bully to the lower school children.

Thomas was the most tormented of all of them—he was small-built for his age, with people usually guessing him to be about ten. His paleness didn't help either, as his bright blonde hair shone for miles creating a beacon for bullies to hone in on the weakest target available. His small frame got pushed around easily, and whenever he spoke, his prepubescent voice would be jeered for its femininity—he was the boy who always had something to say but would never say it for fear of his peers muffled laughter and constant teasing. He had learnt long ago to keep his mouth shut. When he was around nine, turning ten, he had been moved to particularly mean foster parents who would punish him for speaking when not being spoken to, and so had learnt that the best defence was the silent defence.

He eventually moved from there, but no kindness or compassion could change his silence, and he continued to only speak when absolutely necessary, sometimes not even then. He had almost no memory of his biological parents, as they had decided they could not raise a child and so had sent him into foster caring until they felt the time was right (if it ever would be) to take him back again.

The only memory he had of both his parents together was of them reading to him—every night they would bury themselves in one of his favourite books— his absolute favourite had been *The Little Prince* by the famous French aviator and author Antoine de Saint-Exupéry. He could remember their voices as they smoothly read through the comforting words of that great lyonnais novella, "It is only with the heart that one can see rightly, what is essential is invisible to the eye," his hope of reuniting with them was held in that one book which he kept a copy of perpetually under his pillow. At night he would, without fail, turn over to face his window and look up at the stars, knowing that his parents might be looking up at the same stars as he was and that if he thought hard enough about them, perhaps they would be thinking about him also. That was enough to make him smile—to continue running without growing weary.

CHAPTER III

"A rock pile ceases to be a rock pile the moment a single man contemplates it, bearing within him the image of a cathedral."

—*Antoine de Saint-Exupéry, Le Petit Prince*

Just before noon, the boys left their rooms to find the dining hall. They had been left to their own devices since being shown their rooms, and after unpacking had each taken quite a different course of action. Peter decided to go for a walk through the building to orient himself with his surroundings, then went back to his room to quietly flip through a book he had found in the school library, "*The Story of Beatrix Potter: a Biography*". His room comprised of a door at one end and a large Byzantine-arched window at the other, with just enough room for two single beds on either side of the room and a small wardrobe at the foot of each. The window was open with a fresh breeze meandering through. His roommate, who he had not met yet, seemed to keep his half of the room in good condition. Peter had found his roommate's name on a file sitting on the bed opposite him—Jeremy Fisher. For some reason, the name seemed familiar to Peter, but he brushed it off as just being a common name.

People often say there are two types of people in the world, which of course by any division is true. There are those that are right-handed, and those that aren't. There are those that love pineapple on pizza, and those that don't. There are those who are the Monarch of the United Kingdom, and those that certainly are not. The list of ridiculous and trivial divisions go on *ad nauseam*. For of course always those that *are* something and those that *aren't* must be mutually exclusive and fulfil a complete mathematical set. And so it was with Peter and Jack's roommates, there are those that are clean and neat and respectable, and those that aren't. Jack entered his room to find his bed covered in dirty clothes and half eaten packets of food. The teen stench of over-compensatory male deodorant (if you ever work in a high school, you will know this all too well) densely filled the air to the point where Jack coughed and sputtered before opening the stiff and rattly window to let the fresh breeze through, destroying a few spiders' homes in doing so.

He cleared his bed of his comrade's mess and dumped it all on the bed opposite, checking a tag on a shirt which had a name written on it as he did so. "COLE BLACK" the tag stated in heavy block letters. "Well, Cole, things had better change," Jack thought as he opened the wardrobe, finding a collection of bottles half-filled with vodka, cider, and other strong-smelling concoctions. Next to these bottles he found a small pocket knife tucked under a dirty pair of underwear. Right at the bottom of the wardrobe was a collection of photos, sitting on top of a collection of frames. "Guess he had intended to frame these but never did," Jack thought as he picked up the photos and slowly filed through them.

The first was a physically imposing young man with hair as black as shoe polish, in a stance that people stand in when they want to look dominating and masculine. The next one down was a family, again with the boy. He was looking a bit younger this time, a smaller girl and boy standing on either side of him, and two adults (presumably their parents) behind them. Jack had a quick glance at some writing scrawled on the back: "The Black Family with children: L-R: Ebony, Cole, Jet." The third photo in the pile was of a beautiful girl whom Jack would later find to be the belladonna Charmaine du Sabre. And the fourth—oh, hello—Jack recognised this boy standing next to Charmaine with a big goofy grin on his face. It was Lorenz from earlier. The next was one of Cole with his arm around the girl, as if on a first date. At this point, Jack guessed at what the situation might be: Cole was going out with Lorenz's sister. Quickly leafing through the remaining photos, this theory was confirmed. A collection of photos of the du Sabre family and the Black family. But after a few of these congenial portraits the quality turned much more amateur and Jack had to do a double take. What was this? Much to Jack's surprise, a picture of Charmaine scantily clad in just underwear. And then another, and another, and oh, Lord, now she was naked. Jack felt he should look away, but being sixteen and having photos of such beauty in front of you made it easier said than done. He had every intention to stop out of respect for his new room-mate and the girl, but he was frozen *in situ*, and continued flipping now more slowly and pointedly through the many raunchy images.

"I need to stop looking at these," he said to himself. But there were so many, and he was filled with lust over the girl depicted. Surely, Cole wouldn't notice if he took one and slipped it into his pocket? But maybe that would be too risky. It could fall out, so he quickly grabbed one and pushed it down under his belt and into the crotch of his shorts, tucking it into his underwear—it would be safe there. He took a moment to calm down and check that his "excitement" wasn't visible and then put the photos back, deciding that he would pretend as though he had run out of time before lunch to move the junk from the wardrobe. And so he left the alcohol, the knife, and the photos, and sheepishly headed off to find Peter and go to lunch—what had he gotten himself into?

"So, what's your room like?" asked Peter on the way down the stairs.

He thought for a moment, then said, "Yeah, it seems alright. Guy seems a bit messy though, needs to clear out the wardrobe. I think he might be dating Lorenz's sister. Yours?"

"It seems perfectly fine, nice and neat," replied Peter.

The dining hall was a cacophony of sound due to boys from the age of twelve to seventeen running about unsettled after class. The space was filled with round tables in rows all down the hall, each table having eight plastic chairs surrounding them. The twins stood just inside the door looking slightly lost until a man sporting a clerical collar came and shook their hands.

"Welcome, lads. You must be Peter...and you must be Jack." He said, looking at them in turn and getting them the right way around.

"Yes, good guess, sir," Peter replied.

"Oh, it wasn't a guess, boys...and it's 'Father,' not 'Sir'...Father Culpa actually," he said with a smile.

"Now, I have a list of your peer support students. We sit in peer support groups for lunch, you're at table eight. Come, follow me…all those that are heavy luncheoned, and I shall give you rest," he let out a small laugh as if he had just made a joke that very few would understand. He led them to the table and gave them a list, speaking further instructions to ensure they were kind and good role models to the younger boys. "Now, also, after classes today. You'll need to plan a team-building exercise. I'll pop in to make sure everything is going alright. Just organise some sort of fun activity, a basketball game perhaps? You've got quite an interesting group of youngsters, boys. You mainly need to look after young Steerforth, he hasn't settled in very well. And with the others, just remember to be patient and kind. There's no such thing as a bad person, just good people who make bad decisions."

He handed them a sheet of paper with some boring information about the ethos of the school—the usual drivel about inclusion, self-betterment, and "no put-down zones." Then handwritten at the bottom was the list:

"Group 8:
- T. Steerforth—Yr 7
- J. King—Yr 8
- L. du Sabre—Yr 9

- R. White—Yr 9
- B. Gayer—Yr 10
- V. Graves—Yr 10"

And then scrawled on the bottom, almost like a signature: "UIOGD."

"Looks like we have Tom in our group…and Lorenz as well" Peter sighed.

After about a minute sitting there, the final lunch bell rung—the one that told all the students to sit down, and the six little youngins found their way to table eight and their new senior caretakers. After brief introductions, Peter made them all share an interesting fact about themselves with the group. The usual sorts of things came up, for example, "my name's Joe and my favourite food is pineapple pizza," and "my name's Victor and I have a pet cat called Hugo," Then it got to Thomas Steerforth, a boy whom the twins recognised but didn't make a point of.

After an awkward pause and some encouragement from Peter, Tom gathered up the courage to speak.

"My name's Thomas. I'm not very interesting."

"Oh, come now. I'm sure there's something interesting you can say about yourself," Peter said gently.

This time, Lorenz decided to take it upon himself to find the words for Tom. "There sure is. Tom, why don't you tell them about the time you called the Fr.

Culpa 'dad'? Or the time you wet your pants in church? Or the fact that you're an orphan—that's a good one!"

"Lorenz!" Peter scolded. "That isn't necessary, don't be mean."

"I'm just trying to help. He can't seem to get the words out by himself."

"I'm not an orphan. I'm fostered. My parents are alive," Tom said sheepishly.

"Sure, whatever helps you sleep at night, Tommy." Lorenz sneered, at which Jack kicked him under the table.

"Ow! What did you do that for? I'm just helping him. He can't live in a fairy-tale land forever. If his parents loved him they would..."

"Enough!" said Peter. "Next person."

"Okay, *alors*, my name is Lorenz du Sabre and I..." he trailed off, seemingly looking past Peter and Jack to something happening behind them. "And that's my sister...and her boyfriend," he nodded past the twins to the pair walking up to the table.

"*Lorenz, je dois faire semblant de tu dire quelque chose d'important à propos de notre famille,*" Charmaine rapidly spurted on arrival at their table. She needed to pretend that she had news from the family to tell Lorenz, as otherwise she wouldn't be allowed in St. Benedict's to visit Cole.

"Hello, Charmaine," Tom said softly, to which he got some surprised looks and suddenly shrunk into his chair as if he had said a horrific curse word. "Sorry."

"Yeah, whatever, *pourquoi est-ce qu'il me parle? Je dois payer pour mon pain pour le déjeuner. As-tu du changement?*" She asked Lorenz

"Oui, je pense."

"Chouette, merci."

It was a conversation that Peter could only half keep up with because of his limited French. Something about a pine tree farting and an owl?

"So which one of you am I sharing a room with?" asked Cole, almost as if accusing both of them of encroaching on his territory.

"Hi, I'm your new roomie. My name's Jack," he said, standing up and offering an outstretched hand. The hand was left hanging in suspense.

"Okay, can I speak to you privately for a moment?" Jack was now a bit nervous—had he somehow left a clue that he'd seen the photos? Did Cole know about the one he had taken? An intrusively violent strip search flashed through Jack's mind as they walked away from the table to have a chat.

"Now, John,"

"…Jack."

"Yeah, whatever. Let me tell you how things work around here. I've had my own room since the middle of last year. My old roommate got curious and had to leave."

"Got curious…had to leave…what does that mean?"

"Don't you worry about it, bud. Just stay out of my way and I'll stay out of yours, and we'll get along just fine." He put his hand on Jack's shoulder. "You seem like a decent guy so just stay on my good side and we'll be alright."

"Okay, well, why wouldn't I be on your good side?"

"The last guy—well, you see he asked too many questions. Like 'where were you last night,' and 'where did you get that from.' Then, he decided to rummage through my things. So, I got rid of him."

Jack's mouth dried up like a potsherd. Did Cole know what he had been doing before lunch?

"Now, look here, Jake…"

"Jack."

"Yeah. Look here. Sometimes I might not come back to my room at night. You know, it's hard keeping a relationship going over a wall, so we need to take all the opportunities we can get. I'm sure you understand that. Sometimes, maybe I'll have a visitor in my room for the night. Well, in those cases you can find somewhere else to sleep, maybe the bathroom, or make a friend and bunk in their room occasionally." Jack just gaped in confusion—how could he be serious about all this?

"And I see Lorenz is in your peer group. You need to know that boy is very close to my heart, and there is an absolutely disgusting conspiracy within the lower years to pin blame on him for things he hasn't done. Look after him for me, will you, and tell me if anyone is unfair to him. I have my eye on a few of the little runts who think it's okay to get him in trouble. He's a good kid." He seemed to rush through this so that Jack wouldn't question any of it.

"Also, I have a lot of 'stuff'—I'll need some of your wardrobe space, and maybe the area under your bed. Sorry about the state of the room this morning. I was going to clear my clothes off your bed but ran out of time. I'm sure you understand, right?"

You see, Cole was one of those people who thought that the pleasantry of "I'm sure you understand" made anything preceding it acceptable. There are many people who think that—that they can say or do anything and a "you understand right?" or "I hope that's okay?" or "I'm just kidding" makes everything alright. Murder is okay so long as you end it pleasantly, I'm sure my readers will understand *that*? It is often said that how somebody says something is much more important than what they say. Perhaps that is true, or perhaps it is a precarious balance in importance between the two. For no matter how nicely you tell someone that they may have to on occasion sleep in a toilet cubicle, and no matter how many times you surround your dialogue with "chap" or "bud" or pats on the back, it does not make it a nice thing to say, or a reasonable request.

"And what if...well, I guess I'm saying...what if I refuse?" Jack finished with a gulp.

Suddenly Cole grabbed Jack by the collar and pushed him against the wall he was standing against, moving his face so close to Jack's that he could feel his warm breath on his cheek "Then maybe there will be some trouble...and we wouldn't want that, would we."

Jack was usually not opposed to "trouble," and if he was a little bit closer to Cole's build, his reply may have been quite different. However, being the same height but about fifteen kilograms lighter made him rethink his usual response to aggression.

"No, no of course we wouldn't. I think we'll get along just fine," Jack said with a feigned smile.

But Cole had noticed something strange on Jack's person. You see, holding him up by his collar had made his shirt taut from his belt up, and a strange shape appeared in his shirt just above his beltline—one of a corner of a piece of card.

"What's that?" Cole signalled downwards.

"Oh shit," thought Jack. "It's a...ummm...a photo of my mum. She died when I was young so I always keep a photo of her with me."

"Why do you keep it in your pants?"

"Ahhh, well, yes. That's a very good question and there's a very good answer to that."

He had to stop and think for a second, but Cole wasn't going to change the subject.

"It's to keep it safe. You see I'm so useless at not losing things, and in my pocket it might fall out. Or be pick-pocketed, you never know who's around."

"Okay…can I see it?" Cole was still suspicious about the shaky story.

"Well, you see, Cole. I can't let you see it because…"

Suddenly Cole went in for the grab, being overcome with curiosity about what it could be. Luckily, Jack managed to squirm out of position and quickly turned to face the wall.

"Cole!" Fr. Culpa called from a few metres away. "What on Earth are you doing?"

"Nothing, Father. Just welcoming Josh here to the new school. Teaching him the secret room 601 handshake you know?" he pretended to give Jack's hand a friendly little slap. "Anyway, I just finished telling him about your great sermons on Sunday, Father. They really are the highlight of my week."

"Aha, right, well, I think Jack is feeling welcome enough. Perhaps you can go back to your own table now, and thank you for letting me know your appreciation of my sermons. I guess that means I should sign you up for Thursday night bible study?"

"Oh, no, Father, I'm actually busy on Thursday nights. But the moment that changes I will let you know immediately!"

And so Jack escaped the ordeal, quickly returning to their table while Cole and Fr. Culpa continued to play a cat-and-mouse bible study game.

"Peter, you still have a photo of mum in your wallet don't you?" he asked frantically.

"Yes, why?"

"It's a long story, I'll tell you later. But I need to borrow it and put it down my pants. It's important."

Peter looked puzzled but agreed, he was curious about the request but had grown not to question some of Jack's ridiculous ideas. Jack subtly slunk down in his chair so that the table was up to his chest and tried as discreetly as he could to switch the two photos whilst not arousing suspicion. But what to do with Charmaine's photo. There was a backpack under the table and so he unzipped it slightly and shoved it in. "Not my problem now," he thought to himself with a little smirk.

CHAPTER IV

"Therefore, dear Sir, love your solitude and try to sing out with the pain it causes you. For those who are near you are far away . . . and this shows that the space around you is beginning to grow vast..."

—*Rainer Maria Rilke, Letters to a Young Poet*

After lunch, the twins had literature together. A subject that thankfully Cole wasn't smart enough to share with them, for Jack was not looking forward to seeing Cole again, let alone having to spend an entire year sharing a room with him. Peter finally got to meet his new roommate, Jeremy Fisher, and they instantly hit it off with their similar personalities.

The literature teacher, Mrs. Bowen, was the most ancient and wrinkliest lady the twins had ever seen. Lorenz had often said that she was "as old as the rebuilding of Somalia." Her skin reminded Peter of a crocodile leather handbag he had once seen, her permed hair a grey cloud surrounding her balding scalp. The little hairs on her upper lip quivered as she inhaled and exhaled sonorously between the lines of Shakespeare she was reading. The greatest irony of the situation was that she was reading from Shakespeare's sonnet 130—the poem about the ugly mistress. Peter and Jeremy sat there listening with a small amount of interest to the discussion of sonnets. While Jack had more pressing thoughts such as how uncomfortably the corners of the photo prodded into his pelvis, and what his strategy would be that evening when he would have to spend time with Cole, unless he had to sleep in a toilet cubicle, that was.

Literature class seemed to drag on forever—have you heard the Winchester definition of a classic? "A book that everybody wants to say they have read, but that nobody actually wants to read." To Jack, this made every book a "classic" although he had never wanted to say that he had read a book enough to actually read one unless it was forced upon him. He often relied on Peter to give a synopsis of what had happened and was getting ready to ask him for a summary of the lesson, when Mrs. Bowen stopped rambling on and changed her tune to something that Jack suddenly pricked up about.

"Now, gentlemen. The exciting news of the day. The school play." She started in a deadpan voice. "This year we're doing *Romeo and Juliet*, that's by Shakespeare in case you didn't know. Auditions are in a month and we need a strong actor for Romeo, as well as all the other male characters of course. We've precast Juliet, who will be played by Charmaine du Sabre from St. Scholastica's. There is information on the arts board, and a character breakdown for you all. The auditions will be held on Friday after school.

Once the bell went, the exeunt from that classroom was remarkable. You could've blinked an eye and missed twenty or so boys all standing up and leaving. For it was the best time of the day: the largest number of hours of freedom until classes the next day. Peter and Jack both rushed up to their dorms to get changed into their sports uniform ready for the basketball match that they had organised for their peer group. Jack's room was empty and so he got changed in peace—"better slip the photo into these pants and continue the charade," he thought. They reconvened in the hallway ready to go down in their green gym shorts and white polo shirts, once again sporting the school emblem and motto.

"This game has a ninety-nine percent chance of becoming violent, you know?" Jack laughed. "How do we stop Lorenz from knocking Tom's lights out?"

"Easy. We put them on the same team." Peter paused and tapped his head a couple of times. "See, this is why everyone says I'm the older and wiser brother"

"You think that'll stop him?" smirked Jack. "I'll bet he still starts beef, he's a troublemaker."

"Along with his sister and her boyfriend?" Peter enquired

"Well, yes. As a matter of fact, I've only just met him and I don't think that highly of Cole either. In fact, I think he's much worse than Lorenz"

"And Charmaine?"

"Well, I don't know. I've hardly had a chance to meet her now have I?"

"Interesting that she's going to be Juliet, isn't it? You going to audition for the play? Seems like your sort of thing."

"I might just do that, who knows?" Though while he said it, he knew that the answer was that he wanted to be Romeo more than anything else in the world right now. He'd seen the beauty in that photograph and was starting to imagine what being the Romeo to her Juliet would be like.

The basketball match went off as expected. To make teams even, Peter went with three of the younger boys and Jack went with the other three. Lorenz blamed Tom for every small imperfection in the team. Tom didn't argue but meekly accepted his fate of being the team scapegoat and Lorenz's personal punching bag. Naturally, Jack and Peter trash-talked the whole game. Peter's team ended up winning, and the team consisting of Jack, Lorenz, Tom, and Victor lost miserably–a house divided against itself cannot stand. Fr Culpa did as he promised and dropped in for about ten minutes to watch, and of course the boys were on their best behaviour when supervised. Lorenz would offer Tom a high five every few seconds, and nobody would push or shove or cheat. None of this fooled Fr. Culpa who knew the boys well enough to know that the moment he left, they'd turn into savages again, but at least for the time he watched them he could bring some order and dignity into the game before it became akin to a scene from *Lord of the Flies* again.

When the timer that Peter had set on his phone went off to signal half-time, Jack's team was down thirty-two to ten and Lorenz had become visibly frustrated at his team's weak link.

"Can we swap the teams around, Peter? It's not fair. Tom's too weak, *il est faible.* He can't throw the ball hard enough."

"Lorenz. He's trying. Just leave him alone for more than a few seconds. Then maybe he'd be more confident."

"It's not the confidence he doesn't have, it's the muscle. Look at him," Lorenz said accusingly, grabbing Tom's arm to show how weak it was. Tom instantly jerked away and so Lorenz picked up the ball at his feet.

"Look, I'll help him. Here, Tom, this is how you throw a ball. It's not the rocket surgery," he sneered as he threw it full pelt at Tom's face. The thud and bloody nose that followed sent Tom running off crying and Peter hot in pursuit to console him, while Jack was left to chastise Lorenz for his stupidity. Peter caught up with Tom, and fumbling through his pockets, gave him a handful of dirty tissues as they went through the gate out of the basketball court, walking a small distance to sit under a nearby tree.

"I'm sorry that happened to you, Tom. I know it wasn't my fault, but I'm sorry he did it anyway. And besides, I probably should've seen what he was doing and I could have stopped him."

The usual silence from Tom, so Peter decided to continue.

"I know Lorenz bullies you, and I know it's hard to compete against the older, bigger boys. But…but things are going to get better, Tom, I promise. I'm going to make them better for you. If Lorenz bullies you, you just tell me and I'll sort it out, okay?"

"Okay," whispered Tom hoarsely.

"Great, good. I'm glad we had this chat, Tom." Peter slapped him on the back, "Things are going to be better for you from now on."

After about five minutes they went back to playing basketball and Lorenz eased up on the constant sledging. Perhaps, Peter thought, there was some empathy in Lorenz's mean heart after all.

After the match, they all collapsed onto the grass next to the courts, every one of them utterly exhausted from the chaotic and violent match. They were all in good merriment and felt like they had bonded together as a group during the match.

"Did you know there's a sporting competition between different peer support groups here? We should enter," started Adam once they had all caught their breath.

Lorenz was the first to pipe in, as usual. "Yes, we should. And I guess…I guess we're *all* a good team." It almost seemed like he had choked on these last few words, but for once he had complimented the little thorn in his side. But then the temptation was too much and Lorenz couldn't stop himself from continuing. "Except Tom," he said. "We need all strong members and not…"

"Oh, shut up, Lorenz," Peter answered. "What sporting events would we need to train for?"

Adam continued, "It's a pentathlon with basketball, soccer, running, water polo, and wrestling. We could do it."

"That sounds like a possibility. We're all pretty fast and strong," Peter replied. It would, after all, be a very good bonding activity.

"Except…" Lorenz started to mumble.

"Shut it," Jack snapped.

"You know," Joe started at Peter and Jack, "we were interrupted at lunch and you never told us an interesting fact about yourselves. So what brings you guys here? What's your story?"

"Oh, it's complicated, you know? We were going to St. Raymond's College, in the city. But then we were expelled so our dad sent us here. This is our first boarding school experience." Peter replied, trying to avoid details but knowing that he'd be pressed to find out more.

Lorenz, being the curious guy he was, decided to be the one to press for more. "So why were you expelled then? Who did you sleep with? Or, who did you kill… or, or…I bet it was gory!" he said, his eyes opening wide in excitement and intrigue.

"No, no. Nothing like that," Jack answered. "It's just too complicated to go into. It's a long story."

"We have a long time before dinner," Victor smiled.

The rest of the late afternoon was whiled away sharing story after story between themselves. One story is of the utmost importance, and that is the one I will tell you now. The story of what actually happened at St. Raymond's College that led to Peter and Jack's expulsion. See, they had always been seen as trustworthy kids, especially amongst their peers, which often meant that they were privy to the intimate revelations of their friends. They became accustomed to being a listening ear and a shoulder to lean on for their colleagues in times of need. Then one day, Peter read a book about a man who invited strangers to write their deepest, darkest secret down anonymously on a postcard and mail it to his address. He received thousands and thousands of postcards. The rest of the story is irrelevant—something about him going on a quest to find these people and improving their lives and then he drowns in a hotel pool after an accident with a dumbbell and a chain. But from this they gleaned the fact that they could organise and document the secrets that they were being told. So the twins had bought a huge book of empty pages and had invited a few of their close friends to arrange a time where they could tell their secret, under the promise of absolute privacy and discretion that the book would be kept "under lock and key," so to speak. Word got out amongst the school's student body through the omnipresent gossip mill and fairly soon the boys had a booking every night with a peer divulging his most obtrusive lusts, or admitting to his most heinous crimes.

This little arrangement worked well for a couple of months, but as is often the case with precarious situations, the ironic phrase "what could possibly go wrong" comes into mind. The answer is a lot. A lot could possibly go wrong and did go wrong. The staff of St. Raymond's found out about the book and the events that followed saw the twins expelled. Just after their expulsion, Roger heard from a friend of a distant relative about the Draconian discipline of St. Scholastica's and so had resolved to send the boys to St. Benedict's where they might be reformed and directed back onto the right path. Little did he know of the astronomical difference between St. Scholastica's and its brother school. But the twins had promised to behave this time, and they both had every intention of keeping that promise with their father.

The light was beginning to fade as the twins wrapped up their story, and it was almost dinner time so they all stood up and started heading back towards the college building. As they entered the building, Mr. Latan appeared through a doorway with an esky-sized cardboard box, somewhat struggling to carry it around.

"Hi boys, can one of you do a job for me? I need someone to take this to St. Scholastica's – it's not as heavy as it looks."

"Sure, I will," Jack offered. He hadn't been across to the other side and was always happy to go for a walk.

"Great, here you go." Mr. Latan awkwardly transferred the box into Jack's waiting arms. He led Jack out the door and pointed down a footpath to a gate about a hundred metres away. "When you get to that gate," he said, "press the button on the side of the wall and it'll connect to the intercom at St. Scholastica's, and they'll unlock the door for you. Once you're done, come straight back for dinner."

Jack rested the box on the balustrade of the stairs that led to the front door and then fumbled with it to try to work out the best grip on it. He bent down and then rose again. Up got Jack, and off he trot, as fast he could caper…no wait, sorry wrong story. He grasped the box from the bottom and just started walking normally over to the gate. "This definitely IS as heavy as it looks," he thought to himself. He wondered what was in there—a microwave? No, too big. Books perhaps? Maybe an anvil? It felt like it. He noticed, strangely, that scrawled onto it in thick permanent marker was "M. CULPA."

After a brief conversation over the intercom, the gate swung open and he found himself finally on the other side of the red brick wall. The change in scenery struck him at once: manicured gardens with wooden benches and old street lamps like something out of Narnia. No overgrown grass invading the pathways over here.

He ambled towards the towering façade of St. Scholastica's, continually in awe of his beautiful surroundings. The air smelled sweeter over here too, perhaps it was the flowers or perhaps just the lack of boys. He entered into the front office and dropped the box down in front of the cranky-looking admin lady. He was about to start on his way back to St. Benedict's, his stomach telling him it was definitely dinner time, when he heard a voice call out behind him.

"Hey, you," a girl called.

He turned around to see a sandy-blond girl rushing light-footedly down the stairs. He recognised her straight away. "Me?" he questioned.

"Yeah, aren't you Cole's new roommate?" she asked, "or are you his twin?"

"Yeah, that's me, I guess. Why?"

"I'm his girlfriend."

"I know."

"Walk with me," she said, making sure that no-one was around to see her, she led him back out the door and started down the path. "I assume St. Benedict's is expecting you back?"

"Yeah of course—it's dinner time."

"Well—you know the intercom at the gate? It's just an intercom—there's no camera. So I don't suppose you'd mind if I walked through with you when you buzz in?"

Jack thought about it—on the one hand he wouldn't mind walking and talking with her, but on the other hand he didn't want her and Cole making out in his room that night.

"No sorry, I'd better not," he replied as he kept walking. But she kept following, clinging onto his arm.

"Oh, come on, please?"

"No, now I need to get back so please stop grabbing me."

"Not even for a kiss on the cheek?" Charmaine tempted him.

Jack thought on it again—the image of Cole roughing him up, or simply just murdering him, flashed through his mind once more.

"No. Now goodnight." They had reached the gate together and Jack was ready to go home.

"Okay, well thanks anyway. Can I have a hug good-night? Because I won't be able to get one from Cole."

"Okay—just a hug." Jack obliged.

It was a nice hug, and a long hug, and Jack was half reconsidering the offer of a kiss, but they eventually unclasped and wished each other well before Jack pressed the intercom and passed through the gate again. He was just about to click it closed when he looked back one more time and saw Charmaine dangling his phone precariously in front of her, holding on to just one corner of it. He pat his back pocket—dang, she must have grabbed it during the hug.

"Let me through and you can have it back" she smugly smiled.

"Fine." Jack said stubbornly, as he let her through. She gave the phone back to him, leaned in and gave him a small peck on the cheek.

"You're cute when you're confused," she said, and then started walking along the path, leaving Jack gaping at the gate that he was still holding open.

So it followed that there was an awkward tension in room 601 that night when Jack entered the dorm, hardly any words were spoken between the two boys. When it came time to get ready for lights out, Jack made sure that Cole was watching him get undressed for bed, so that the photo of his mother could "accidentally" fall onto Cole's bed as he pulled his shorts down to his feet.

"Oh, sorry about that." Jack started. "Just that picture of my mum I was telling you about earlier," to which Cole only made a small grunt of acknowledgement with a distinct absence of words, and then switched off the light to sleep.

Meanwhile, Peter had taken it upon himself to go and talk to Lorenz in his room about his actions earlier in the day.

"You know, he really does get upset about how you treat him," Peter began. "Why do you have to be so mean to him."

"He doesn't mind it," Lorenz replied. "It's like the water off a fish's back. He probably finds it funny."

"Water off a duck's back, Lorenz, a *duck's* back. And he doesn't find it funny, and neither does anyone in the group. You don't need to show off to us. We know you're bigger than him."

Lorenz was silent.

"Well, try to be nice to him and then we'll like you a lot more. Don't be mean just to impress a few stupid kids." Peter felt like he at least had started to get through to Lorenz on this, perhaps he could make a difference to the young boy's way of thinking.

As the moon rose higher in the cloudy sky, the school assumed its usual eerie silence. All was still apart from the birds flapping in the air above, others nesting in the trees ready for night.

"Perhaps these new boys will stop the others from bullying me," Thomas thought as he dozed off, thinking what a great afternoon he had had. He turned to look out the window, from which he could see a single tree on a hill, with a bench under it facing to overlook the forest about a hundred metres from the school. He looked up at the stars and they seemed to glisten more brightly that night, twinkling especially for him. He shifted his focus to the distant St. Scholastica's where he could see a few of the girls' bedroom lights still on. He focused on one in particular. "I wonder how far away that is?" he asked himself. As he watched the meandering breeze blow the glistening pine needles in the moonlight, he slipped into a deep and comfortable sleep. The world, for once, made a little more sense to him.

CHAPTER V

"All happy families are alike; each unhappy family is unhappy in its own way."

— *Leo Tolstoy, Anna Karenina*

The interesting thing with identical twins is that, even though they may be physically identical, they are often far from identical in mind and personality. Although Peter and Jack were difficult—if not impossible—to tell apart if you didn't know them well, their habits and way of doing things could quickly alert you to who was who. Peter had always leaned towards being more patient, thoughtful, and pedantically careful, while Jack tended to charge head first into things, often ignoring details and making mistakes. He didn't even notice the night before that he had set his alarm clock far too early.

Thus, the still empty silence of the school was disturbed by Jack's alarm blaring its merry way through whatever insipid and formulaic rubbish was on the radio at the ungodly hour of five a.m., startling him so much that he awoke having no idea that he wasn't at home. In the confusing darkness, he lurched the way he would at home to switch the alarm off, thereby falling out of his new bed in a knot of sheets and hitting the floor like a sack of potatoes. All of which woke Cole from his slumber, who was none too happy to be disturbed at that time.

"Idiot," he muttered as he picked up a book from his bedside table and threw it square at Jack's head, then rolled over to try to get back to sleep.

Perhaps one of the best feelings in the world (apart from going to the toilet after a long day of holding one's bladder) is the feeling of waking up early and realising you can go back to sleep. This was not Cole's way of thinking as he still had two hours of sleep left to his disposal and was not what would you would call a "morning person." Each morning the college schedule was the same: a wakeup call was put over the P.A. at seven o'clock with notices read out by Mr. Latan each morning in the most dreary and disinterested voice you have ever heard. You know, the usual things that people just can't muster the enthusiasm to care about at that time of the morning—what time choir's on, which group is on lunch clean-up duty, the bible verse for the day—that sort of thing. Morning exercise was then done to the prerogative of the sports teacher, Mr. Coubertin, which usually just consisted of a jog or a swim in the pool that sat next to the dividing wall, but sometimes if Mr. Coubertin felt ambitious, team sports or competitive challenges would be organised. This was always followed by a half hour to shower and prepare for the day, and then breakfast was served at half past eight. Woe to you if you weren't ready for breakfast exactly on time—the doors would be locked precisely on the school bell tower's chime of half past and you would go hungry until lunch.

This is where we begin our next scene, with Jack and Peter sitting with their group at 8:28 am waiting for the breakfast bell to ring and for the refectory doors to be closed. The twins had subtly walked past the serving area and spied a hearty collection of breakfast foods. Their stomachs were rumbling after a particularly stressful relay race earlier that morning, and as usual, Peter was impatiently "watch watching"—that annoying habit your brain has of making you repeatedly look at a clock every couple of seconds without even acknowledging the time. Peter perpetually felt a sense of urgency over the passage of time, feeling uncomfortable if he felt he wasn't spending his time wisely, but then often not doing anything to ease that discomfort. The bell rang on the dot of 8:30 am and the whole group was there, all except for Tom. After a short discussion, the general consensus was that Tom hardly ever missed breakfast and that Peter should go and ask Tom's roommate where he might be.

"Hello, my name's Peter. You're Thomas Steerforth's roommate, yes?" he asked the average-looking boy at table fourteen.

"Yes, James Copperfield's the name," the boy answered with a lilting Irish accent.

"He isn't at breakfast, have you seen him this morning?"

"Yeah, don't worry. He's not dead at the bottom of the pool or in a ditch or anything. He slept in. Even missed morning exercise. He stayed up late last night, drawing."

"Drawing?"

"Oh, yeah, he spends hours drawing. Lots of sketches."

"What does he draw?"

"I'm not sure really. I don't pay much attention to it. I don't see *what* he's drawing, I just see that he *is* drawing."

Peter thought this an interesting distinction that young James had made and so decided to probe further.

"You've never asked him? Aren't you curious?"

"Well, yes, I guess. But I try not to associate with him—you know, he's not very popular. I don't dislike him though, we get along alright. Just not in public, you know."

Peter had stumbled upon a great human curiosity: popularity. A potentially poisonous notion that has led many people to ruin. I'm sure if interviewed more fully, James would admit that he found Tom a more likeable person than Lorenz, and much more likeable than Cole. It's often you'll find the most popular people are not only not the most liked of people, but the most disliked of them. That is the funny thing about popularity—the multitude come to see an illusion created by those more powerful to suppress people that are much more likeable than themselves. If Cole didn't have popularity, what did he have going for him, apart from a beautiful girlfriend?

Peter returned to his table and told the group that Tom had slept in, deciding against divulging the information of Tom's drawing to the group. He had enough going against him, Lorenz and his cronies didn't need any more material. They ate breakfast while talking about the usual topics of schoolboys: what they thought of the teachers, which girls they thought were "hot," and which boys were sneaking over the wall at night. Jack had begun to grow an affection towards Charmaine, as he had figured out that he could look at the stash of photographs any time that Cole wasn't in the room and had taken full advantage of this. But this was not appropriate breakfast conversation, especially with Lorenz at the table. Rather, the conversation moved to Lorenz and his "female interest," and this is where we meet another of our major players in the strategic game of the schools.

You see, Cole had a younger sister, Ebony Black. She was a pale girl with long, black, wavy hair and square glasses. She was neither overly attractive nor overly unattractive. She was the same age as Lorenz, fourteen, and was madly in love with him. He was always polite to her because, of course, he saw her as a future sister-in-law, but was otherwise blind (or, at least, pretending to be blind) to her affections. In other words, he fit into that large swath of humanity that gets trapped in an awkward situation. He was not interested in her at all, but neither did he show any animosity towards her. She was a soft-spoken and delicate girl who would never say anything to hurt anyone—the type of girl who wears floral dresses and has an interest in photography. Everybody was nice to her, partly out of fear of Charmaine, but also partly because there was nothing to be mean to her about. One could say that she had similar characteristics to Tom, but that the way boys treat an outsider is much different to the way that girls treat one. She was able to get away with just being generally ignored and left in peace to smell the flowers and walk through the forest alone, dismissed simply as "quirky."

Everybody who knew both Cole and Ebony wondered how two parents could produce two such different children, but in truth they were not actually all that different. She was the image of what Cole had been in his younger years. Ebony still had fond memories of going butterfly catching with him (releasing them unharmed afterwards, of course), and taking long walks through the forest, piggy-backing on him when her frail legs became tired. On Christmas mornings, they had always woken each other up and raced down to watch the other's face when opening their present. Every summer, they would go on a roadtrip with the family: Cole, Ebony, their parents, and their younger brother Jet who was a full nine years younger than Cole. Many fond memories swirled around Ebony's mind of yesteryear. Somewhere they also swirled around in the back of Cole's mind, but they were becoming more and more trapped and surrounded by other thoughts. At about the age of twelve, Cole had stopped wanting to spend time with his sister. He grew up and found what he thought better ways to occupy his time: video games, girls, and other things of dubious productivity. So Ebony fell by the wayside, and you can trust me when I say butterfly hunts aren't half as fun on your own.

Somewhere there was a little child inside Cole that wanted to go and grab Ebony's hand and take her for a long walk through the gardens of the schools. But his pride was too great, and it would be an embarrassment for him to speak more than a few sentences to Ebony each time they met. That isn't to say he didn't love her or that she wasn't important to him. More so that he *intended* to be a good brother, but without even realising it, continually failed miserably at that endeavour. His intentions were there, but his actions were not. Ebony understood it all quite well, knowing that he had a group of friends that would give him flak for spending time with his sister. "He's not a bad brother," she would say to herself, "just a good brother that makes bad decisions because of other people."

Funnily enough, these were the exact words that Jack often thought about Peter and that Peter often thought about Jack, especially when Jack did stupid things like deciding to change the subject from Ebony and Lorenz to another couple of people.

"So Lorenz, what is Charmaine and Cole's relationship like? Like honestly? I can't imagine they're doing too good. They just seem like such different people."

There was a long silence where you could almost be forgiven for thinking we were viewing a silent movie. Everybody at the table just stared at Jack in disbelief that he would ask such a question.

"I mean, maybe that came out the wrong way. I mean…are they happy with each other? She's such a lovely person and he's…"

"They're fine." Lorenz retorted, looking personally offended that his sister's judgement might not be perfect. "They say the opposites attract, don't they?"

"Yes, sometimes they do, I guess…for some time."

Peter gave Jack the most belligerent look he could muster, and then politely excused himself and Jack to go get some more breakfast.

"Do you have a death wish?" Peter asked. "You know he's going to go straight up to Cole or Charmaine and regurgitate exactly what you just said? And then, well, you're the one sharing a room with Cole. Good luck with not being murdered in your sleep. Have fun with that…idiot."

"She deserves better." Jack shook his head, piling up some more muesli into his bowl. "He's an animal, she's beautiful and elegant and sweet and…"

Peter's eyes widened as he realised what was happening. "You've met her once, you moron. You can't tell me you're in love with her."

"I'm not saying that. I'm just saying from what I've seen, he doesn't deserve her."

"And you'd be a better match for her I guess?"

"I didn't say that. Stop putting words in my…" At this point, Jack realised just how much breakfast Peter was piling on for seconds. "You're going to eat all that?"

"No, I'm going to smuggle it out and take it up to Tom. It's the least we can do. He might be feeling upset about the basketball incident yesterday. Anyway, my point is to just go easy on the Charmaine-Cole relationship. They're together. Just calm your pants and focus on your school work."

"Geez, yes, Dad. With all this mollycoddling of Tom you'd think *you're* the one that's in love."

"Don't start with me or I'll call up Dad straight away and tell him what a pain you're being, Jack."

At this point, Jack showed his greatest theatrical skill. Although, perhaps it's not really a skill when you're imitating an identical twin. It can't be that difficult really, can it?

"Don't start with me or I'll call up Dad straight away and tell him what a pain you're being, Jack," Jack mimicked, using the brattiest voice possible while pretending his hand was a telephone.

"I will, I'm serious."

"Whatever." Jack dismissed him as he walked back to the table.

Meanwhile, Peter looked around and then stealthily ducked through a backdoor with the plate stacked high with breakfast for Tom, climbing the stairs still paranoid that a teacher might've seen what he was doing.

"Peter!" A voice echoed out from behind him. It was Father Culpa who happened to have been walking past the foot of the stairs. He was caught red-handed.

"It's for Tom. He didn't make it to breakfast on time."

"I know. But you forgot a spoon for his cereal," the priest held out a spoon for Peter. "You think I would stop someone from feeding the hungry? Go and be careful not to let anyone see you." He gave Peter an understanding nod to which Peter returned a nod of admiration, then continued on his way to the dining hall while Peter continued up the stairs.

"Oh, and Peter." The boy turned around. "*Ad Maiorem Dei Gloriam.* Don't forget to have a good day."

And that was all they said that morning.

CHAPTER VI

"Let no one who loves be called altogether unhappy.
Even love unreturned has its rainbow."

— *J.M. Barrie, The Little Minister*

O n arrival at the dorm, Peter knocked on the
door and called out Tom's name, which was
answered with a weak and nervous "who is it?"

"It's Peter. I brought you breakfast. Can I come in?"

"Hold on a second." Then a rustle of papers from
inside and a drawer being slammed, after which Peter
was allowed to enter. He passed the plate to Tom and
then sat on the edge of the bed awkwardly while Tom
began to sheepishly eat.

"Nice day today, shame you slept through most
of it," Peter said jokingly, trying to break the awkward
silence that was punctuated only by Tom's chewing.

No answer from Tom, so Peter continued, knowing full well what the rustling papers and slammed drawer would have been.

"Someone told me you like drawing?"

Tom stopped eating, his spoon half way between the bowl and his mouth. He uttered the first truly audible words that Peter had heard from him. "Who told you that?"

"James did. I asked him where you were. We got talking and he said you like drawing."

"Oh, he did? Did he say what I draw."

"No, he didn't know." Peter said, at which point Tom began eating his porridge again. After a few more awkward moments he continued. "What do you draw?"

"Nothing," Tom answered, dismissing it as a silly question.

"You draw nothing? Well, I don't know why you had a late night then. Doesn't take long to draw nothing. In fact, I'm drawing nothing right now aren't I?" Peter quipped, not taking into account that "great artisans" like John Cage have done much more ridiculous things than *drawing* nothing.

"Well, I draw *something*. Why do you want to know?"

"Why wouldn't I want to know, and why wouldn't you want to tell me?"

"Because it's weird."

"What's wrong with weird? Just look at my brother." Peter's attempt at humour once again fell on deaf ears.

"It's just too hard to explain, it would take too long. And you don't want to know about me. I'm not your problem."

"I sure do want to know about you, Tom. I'm really interested in what you're drawing." Peter assured him, very sincerely.

"If people find out, I'll be bullied even more."

"I promise I won't tell a single soul. You can trust me. I can help you. I want to stop Lorenz and all the others from bullying you. I'm on your side, you know that."

At this, Tom had to think for a while, and then reluctantly opened his top drawer, pulling out a stash of papers and handing them to Peter who then slowly flipped through them.

"Are all of these..." Peter paused, choosing his words carefully. "Are all of these Charmaine?"

He continued to flick through almost a hundred sheets of paper. "So, you really like her, huh?"

"Yes, she's perfect . . . well, at least I think she is," Tom shrugged.

At this revelation, a sequence of possible outcomes flashed through Peter's mind. None of them a good outcome. What if Cole found out? What if Lorenz found out? What if Charmaine found out?

"You know, Tom. I think you should hide these somewhere. You don't need to be thinking about this sort of thing."

"Why not? We might end up together. She'll realise that she's too good for Cole, and then I'll have a chance. I can already tell she likes me."

Peter didn't know where to start explaining all the things wrong with these assertions. The fact that Tom thought he had any chance in the entire history of the cosmos of ending up with Charmaine was baffling to Peter, but he couldn't bring himself to break the young boy's heart. "Well, I guess anything is possible," he reluctantly answered.

"You think it's crazy, don't you?" Tom sighed. "I knew I shouldn't have told you. I knew nobody would think I have a shot with her."

Peter thought for a little while, knowing that he would have to choose his words carefully.

"Tom. There's nothing crazy about having feelings for someone. No matter who it is, you can't help who you become attracted to so don't be embarrassed about it. It's part of life."

"That's not all. That's just the start of it." Tom stopped for a moment while he mustered up the courage to ask his next question. "You know how you said you used to write down people's secrets? Will you write down mine? I want you to understand."

Peter weighed it up in his head and made a quick decision. With Tom's permission, he went to stealthily grab his laptop from his room and returned, poised on James' bed and ready to type. Many years after the events in this book took place, and after a diligent search of all the evidence presented, I was able to find the exact transcript of what Peter wrote. This is it, word for word and unedited.

"SECRET OF THOMAS STEERFORTH – COLLECTED ON WEDNESDAY 08/05/2019 @ ST. BENEDICT'S COLLEGE.

I was put into foster care when I was three years old and it's all I've ever known. I got a nice family who had wanted to foster a child because they were unable to have children of their own. My new parents' names were Bill and Nancy and they looked after me very well, loved me like I was actually their son. We lived happily in the city for almost six years.

Then one night a few weeks after my sixth birthday, Nancy sat me down and told me that they would be putting me back into the fostering system again. She told me of how she had fallen in love with another man, much younger than Bill, who she loved very much, and that she was going to leave Bill. She told me that it would be impossible for me to stay with them once they divorced and went their separate ways. I cried all night when I found out, unsure of what would happen to me or what my future would be like.

So I was given over to another couple, this time a couple that lived on a farm just a few blocks from here. Their names were Micah and Alice. They never did any farming though, just let their fields become overgrown with neglect and grass while they drove into the city each day for work. Such a waste of fertile land. They were obsessed with money, and although they'd never admit it, I think they adopted me only for the fostering allowance they could get.

I learnt to organise myself. They often left early in the morning and returned late in the evening, leaving me a list of chores to complete once I got home from school. I hardly even saw them. I would trudge along the highway each morning for over an hour to get to school. Each day on the way to Stapleton Community College I would walk past the towering monoliths of St. Benedict's and St. Scholastica's, wondering what went on in two such grandiose buildings.

Then one day on my way to school, I heard a noise as I walked past the fence of St. Scholastica's. It was a girl ushering me over, a girl with the most beautiful sandy blonde hair and green eyes. Her delicate

French accent to accompany her smooth and caress-
ing voice. It was love at first sight. She asked me what
my name was and whether I could help her. Well, of
course I agreed. She had been walking along the fence
line when she saw a sunbed mattress on the side of the
highway.

She explained to me that her brother was very
sick and that she needed to get him medicine, but the
school wouldn't let her leave, so she was planning a
way to escape. She couldn't get over the spiked top of
the fence without putting something on it first. So I
picked up the mattress and slipped it through the
fence, and she threw it on top. I tried to create a stirrup
with my hands for her to step up onto—I was still only
nine and so small that I couldn't support her anyway,
but she managed to scramble over.

She told me about her brother's liver condition
and that she needed alcohol to kill the virus in his liver.
I told her about the stash of spirits my parents kept, so
we rushed back to my house where we went through
the alcohol collection. She ended up taking a lot, as
much as her bag could carry, saying that it would keep
him well for many weeks.

She thanked me with a kiss on the cheek and ruf-
fled my hair, saying how cute I was, and then left again.
I was in heaven the rest of the day. I didn't even go to
school as by that point I was running so late anyway.

That night, my parents went down into the cellar to select their drink for the night and found eight bottles missing. They got angry with me so I told them exactly what had happened. I thought there was no way they could be angry as I had potentially saved someone's life. Well, they thought my story was ridiculous—helping a girl escape a school, a liver disease—and it suddenly dawned on me that the story did seem a little bit contrived. Micah worked himself up into a rage over it calling me a liar and a useless idiot. They searched all through my room and the house and couldn't find the missing bottles. I was grounded and they never trusted me again.

I didn't see Charmaine for over a year after that, but every time I walked past St. Scholastica's the memory of her face and voice, and of that kiss, would come flooding back. I was as in love as a nine-year-old could be. Or at least, I was in love with the idea of love. And then it dawned on me—the chapel at St. Scholastica's was open for a service every Sunday morning, and everybody was welcome. So early one morning I put on my Sunday best, which really consisted of nothing very special, wrote a note to my 'parents' who were still asleep, and set off on my way to St. Scholastica's.

I sat at the back and spent most of the service scanning the crowd for her, but being predominantly teenage girls, she was hard to find. My eyes then spotted her around the middle row, so I rushed up to her after the service to tell her I always thought about her and could never forget that morning we spent together. The reception was cold. She seemed to not even remember me, and had a confused look when I asked her whether her brother was doing okay. She rushed away before I could tell her who I was.

Still, I decided to go to St. Scholastica's the next week, and the next, and the next. I went every Sunday for about six months, always sitting in the back row and making a quick exit at the end of the service, never trying to speak to her again. But at least I got to see her from as close as a few metres away. It was the highlight of my otherwise dreary and insipid week. On my way out, I would often say a few words to Father Culpa, like 'great sermon,' or 'I liked the bible reading today,' and then rush out so that Charmaine couldn't catch up with me.

He obviously saw the sense of urgency and anxiety in my face week by week, and one week he invited me to morning tea in the rectory after mass. How he had the time for that I'll never know, but he's always been a man who had time for anybody who needed it. We had morning tea and chatted about my life at home and my foster situation. I gave him my home phone number and he said he would call in from time to time to see how everything was going. I told him how much I would love to study at St. Benedict's, but didn't mention that the main reason for that wanting was to be close to Charmaine.

Well, he did more than 'call in'—a few months later, Father Culpa turned up at my door. He went into the study with my parents and they talked for hours. I now assume he was trying to convince them to pay the hefty school fees of St. Benedict's, because when the three of them exited the study, they told me that I would be starting at St. Benedict's for the next term. I was over the moon. Now I could practically live with Charmaine. Micah and Alice also seemed happy for me. I guess they finally saw my education as more important than money.

The first room they gave me faced towards the forest, so I said I didn't feel comfortable with my new roommate so I could be moved to a room that looks towards St. Gertrude's. See over there? That's Charmaine's room, I can see just over the wall and can see if her light is on or off. I've even pieced together a schedule of her classes from things that have come up between people in casual conversation. I've tried extra hard in French class so that I can impress her. *Je pratiquons mon verbe tous la soirs.* One day, she's going to wake up to the fact that Cole is a horrible person and she'll leave him. He's cheating on her anyway, so maybe I'll even expose him for that. I've started lifting weights in the morning so I can be strong enough to stand up to him if he gets aggressive. My life's going to get better. I'm going to make it so."

Peter finished typing and the gravitas of the situation dawned on him. A twelve-year-old child pined over the heart of a seventeen-year-old woman. A child so delusional that in his own mind he not only had a chance with her, but was already only one step away from being with her. Worse still, he was a child who had engineered the last three years just to be near her. For those of us well-versed in Latin, I'm sure the phrase *"vanitas vanitatum"* springs to mind. Or perhaps for us better at English, a three letter acronym involving an explicative may be more suitable. As for Peter, he was completely lost for words. So many questions but where to start? After a few long moments of silence, he finally decided to ask his most burning question.

"Why do you think he's got another girl?"

"I have photos and videos of him going down to the gap in the wall late at night and meeting up with a dark-haired girl. Sometimes they stay by the wall and sometimes she comes in to St. Benedict's with him. But never the other way around, in case Charmaine sees him."

By this point, alarm bells were going off in Peter's head like a fire station. Not only had he geared his life to be with her, he was now stalking her boyfriend.

"Tom, I think you need to get your mind off Charmaine and Cole for a little while. Why don't you try and focus on something else for a little bit?"

Peter decided to confide all of this information in Jack—he was his twin after all, they shared everything. Jack was of course naturally very interested in this, seeing as how he so longed for Charmaine as well, and he read Tom's story word for word.

"You will keep this a secret, won't you Jack?" confirmed Peter.

"Yes. Yes, of course." Jack promised.

But the promises of young men are often ill-thought out, plagiaristic, and marred with obvious suppression. You've probably all heard of the story of the young man whose father went away on a long boat voyage. Before going away, he told his son to be a good person, even giving him ten specific instructions to which the son promised to obey. I forget what they were, but the point is that the son almost immediately started disobeying as soon as his father left. The rest of the story goes as you would expect: something about the son still waiting for his father…

The next few days went by fairly uneventfully. Peter and Jack continued to become closer with their group. The week dragged on with boring literature readings, endless mathematical calculations, and tedious historical event memorising amidst a rising sense of anticipation for the *Romeo and Juliet* auditions later in the week. All looked forward to the slight reprieve that the weekend would bring.

CHAPTER VII

"I took a test in Existentialism. I left all
the answers blank and got 100."

—*Woody Allen*

J ack cleared his throat and gazed up into the expansive darkness ahead of him.

> *"There was a young man who said, God*
> *Must think it exceedingly odd*
> *If he finds that this tree*
> *Still continues to be*
> *When there's no one about in the Quad"*

"Yes, very good reading Jack, thank you." Ms. Bowen yelled from the back row of the theatre. "Next!"

Jack peered out into the darkness, squinting due to the heat of the lights burning his eyes. "But Miss, don't you want to hear more? I can do really good dirty talk for Juliet."

"No…no, please, Jack. Please don't. You don't need…"

"Miss…just have a listen, please." Jack cut in, clearing his throat and half yelling. "Graze on my lips, and if those hills be dry, stray lower, where the pleasant fountains…"

"Jack!" Ms Bowen yelled. "Somebody, get him off the stage."

"But Miss, we haven't done the kissing audition. I think Charmaine and I should try it," Jack pleaded as another boy ushered him off the stage.

"Next auditionee," Ms. Bowen looked at the page and sighed. "Another Lapin. Okay, Peter, make it quick."

"Yes, Miss. I will. Thank you for this opportunity. My poetry reading is also a limerick, and it comes from Ronald Knox."

"Dear Sir, your astonishments odd:
I am always about in the Quad.
And that's why the tree
Will continue to be,
Since observed by, Yours faithfully, GOD."

"Thank you, Peter, but you look and sound exactly like Jack and we can't have two Romeos. Next!"

And as quickly as that, the acting ambitions of the twins were dashed. But that is not particularly interesting to our story as this is not a memoir of their rise to theatrical fame. The more interesting thing was the scene that Peter found when he walked out of the theatre. See, Cole had heard Jack's comment about kissing and he wasn't very happy about it. He had once again cornered Jack in an intimidatingly small space and looked like he was about to take a swing, in fact it appeared that Jack's desperate ramblings of acquittal were revving Cole up more and more.

At the very moment Peter had walked through the door, Tom, who had been on the other side of the room minding his own business, decided Jack needed help. He threw the apple he was halfway through eating straight at Cole and hit him square on the back of the head. The chaos that ensued was tumultuous. Cole looked like he was literally going to end Tom's life and so in a moment of blurred heroism, Jack tried to wrestle Cole to the ground. Tom bolted, with Lorenz hot on his trail under a very quick and angry order from Cole.

Although nimble, Tom's small frame was no match for Lorenz's athleticism and he caught up with Tom just outside the front of the building, tackling him from behind and briefly grappling until he had Tom pinned down in the dirt.

"Please, Lorenz, just let me go before Cole gets here," Tom begged.

Lorenz just smirked. "Why would I do that?"

"Because…because I know you're a good person. You don't really want to hurt me."

Lorenz looked sceptical and it was clear that that approach wasn't going to work.

"And most of all I know you don't actually like Cole. And you think Charmaine deserves better. Please."

Lorenz loosened his hold on Tom. This last statement had gotten to him, but then he tensed again and wound back his fist, delivering an almighty blow which resulted in a solid thud. But he had not hit Tom, he had punched the dirt next to his head so that it would seem to Cole that it had come to blows.

"Take your shirt off and give it to me. Quickly." Lorenz looked around worryingly as Tom obliged. "I'll rub it in the dirt and show it to Cole as evidence that I got you but you slipped away."

"Now go. Run as fast as you can." Tom tried to give him a quick hug but he was pushed away. Lorenz knew he might regret his mercy. He looked at his fist and noticed his knuckles had started to bleed. Exactly the effect he had been aiming for.

To help take the boys' minds off things, Peter organised a games night in the common room for that evening, it being a Friday night they could stay up as late as they wanted. But as they wound their way through the corridors between the dining hall where they'd been having dinner, and the common room, Jack heard a small tapping sound on one of the windows that they walked past. He looked out and saw Charmaine ushering him out and mouthing the words "come out here." He looked ahead of him: he was at the back of the group and no one had noticed that he'd stopped. He guessed he could oblige, so he turned back and went out to see her.

"Have you seen Cole?" Charmaine asked—not exactly the question Jack had hoped for.

"No, I haven't got a clue where he is. Why?"

"We were going to go watch the sunset together, but we're going to miss out if he doesn't turn up soon. We were going to meet under the apple tree but . . . "

"Watch the sunset together? Lame." Jack said discardingly. "You can't even see it from here, the trees are in the way."

"Come with me." Charmaine smiled, half dragging him away by his arm.

She led him back inside the building, and swiftly up the stairs to the third floor, the top one. They weaved through a few corridors and into a storeroom with spare blankets and pillows where she pointed up to a loose ceiling panel. Upon climbing one of the racks, she pushed up and entered the roof-space, with Jack hot on her trail. They ducked and dodged through rafter after rafter and beam after beam until Charmaine opened a small door that lead onto a narrow walkway running between the crenulations and roof of the college.

"Here we are," she said as she sat down between two of the crenulations.

Jack looked in awe out onto the landscape that surrounded the college, the sun wasn't far from setting and had splashed beautiful, soft hues of gold across the grounds of the college. The long shadows of trees stretched all the way to the building. They were high enough above the trees to see the lake behind the college sparkling azurely in the setting sun, and to the East, the girls' college sitting in the middle of its manicured gardens.

"It's beautiful, isn't it?" Charmaine asked. "Cole and I come up here often—it's good to get away from everyone down there."

"Yeah, it's really nice." Jack said awkwardly. "But does Cole like it? I can't imagine him spending the time to watch the sunset."

"Well, he likes it up here because I'm up here— I'm not sure if he cares that much about the sun." She seemed to taper off at this, a sound of sadness crept into her voice. There were a few seconds silence before Jack spoke again.

"You're not really that into Cole, are you? You and him are so different."

Charmaine sighed. "Well, yes, we're very different. He's a bit rough on the surface but he really is a good guy. And for now I'm happy to be with him."

"For *now*?"

"Well, I can't imagine spending my whole life with him, though he seems to think we should."

They sat there looking out over the sun-kissed landscape for a few minutes enjoying each other's company in golden silence until Jack finally summoned up the courage to ask his next question.

"There must be a reason you brought me up here. Do you want to kiss?"

Charmaine screwed up her face "No—just because I said I didn't want to spend my whole life with Cole doesn't mean I want to kiss you."

"Oh, sorry." Jack started fidgeting with his fingers. "I didn't mean to offend you."

"That's okay—I guess I'm just worried that people assume that because I'm with Cole, I'm open for anything." She let out a little laugh. "I guess my biggest fear is that people will associate me with him my whole life."

"My biggest fear is that we're just made-up characters in someone's head. Have you ever thought about that? What if we're just part of some novel or play or movie that someone's writing? And our fates are sealed in the pages of a book? How do we know we even exist outside of that book? Or that our names and actions don't have hidden meanings behind them?" Jack looked down in embarrassment—he was so nervous and awkward that he'd started babbling.

"That's so random, Jack. That'd be one boring book." She laughed again; her face looked even more beautiful in the fading golden light. "What would even happen?"

"Well, I don't know," replied Jack. "I guess what happens in most books: a love triangle, a confrontation, someone'll probably end up dead, probably the most loveable character? I know it probably sounds stupid."

"Yeah, it does." Smiled Charmaine. "But it's ok to be stupid sometimes, isn't it? Anyway, it's getting dark. We should probably go back now." So they made their way back down, Charmaine went to find Cole and Jack went to the Common Room to join in his group's festivities.

The event flew by in the usual way that fun things happen. They played many games like Monopoly, Risk, Cards, and Charades from seven p.m. until around midnight, by which point all the boys in the peer group were so tired that they decided to sleep together in the common room.

It's often said that ninety percent of fun things happen after midnight. Being an innocent young Christian man, I naturally have no idea what *they* are talking about apart from harmless frivolity and unhindered euphoria such as a board game night. Many of my fondest memories have been those late nights of ridiculous silliness. I find it impossible to even explain the astounding contradiction of the whole situation. The most consequential time of your life is probably night-time: a time which decides how productive you will be during the day, and yet those nights of throwing away any worldly consequentialism are sometimes the memories that stick with you and define your experience as a human being, when you're happy just to be a human, uninhibited by any social constructs that exist during the day. When you're perfectly content with being silly, frivolous, and inconsequential.

We unceasingly search for those moments of euphoria, and then when they end, sometimes we are so overcome with nostalgia that we wish they had never happened at all. To me, talk of late-night gatherings conjure up a somewhat Gatsby-esque picture—cigar smoke blanketing the air, empty cocktail glasses strewn around the room, exhausted party-goers strewn with them, and

Debussy's "Clair de Lune" (or some other melancholic tune) wafting through the air from an old gramophone. Of course, this is nothing like what the boys experienced. As the clock ticked over to midnight, the boys remained slumped in their chairs with a couple sprawled on the floor. No alcohol or cigars were had and yet they seemed drunk on life, *la joie de vivre*.

I'm sure you know the old riddle: what do syntactic independence, transcending existence, the magnitude of a real number, and a 17th century architectural style all have in common? Well, I absolutely don't know the answer but it's definitely something to look into. All we need to know is that conversations went into the early hours of the morning, by which time all the boys were dozing off and ended up sleeping in the common room that night.

"Peter…"

"Peter…"

Jack suddenly jolted up from his position on the lounge chair, being vigorously shaken by Tom.

"I'm not…" he started, but then he paused. What did Tom want to tell Peter that he wouldn't want to tell Jack? "Yeah…what?"

"Come with me," Tom replied.

Jack loved a good bit of intrigue and so he obliged, being careful not to wake Peter with whom he'd been tangled up with head-to-tail on the lounge chair.

"Where are we going?" Jack asked, still blurry eyed and disoriented.

"I need to show you something"

"Oh, okay," Jack agreed, being pulled along by the arm by the smaller boy.

They weaved through corridors until they reached the entrance hall. Jack paused to try and read the time on the great grandfather clock that stood there, but through the shroud of darkness he couldn't even make out the hands. Out they went through the front door and down towards the lake. It seemed oddly dark outside, like the moon had disappeared from the sky and the stars had decided not to shine.

"Where are you taking me? It's freezing, I want to go back." Jack complained.

"Just keep walking," Tom said, dismissing his complaints.

As they neared the lake, Jack could just make out a solitary silhouette in the darkness. He squinted, trying to make out the broad-shouldered figure. When he stopped squinting, he realised Tom was no longer with him. "Tom?" he whispered, turning around this way and that—no response. He was now all alone in the almost pitch black, the only sentient being he shared the cold darkness with was the man facing the lake, so he decided to continue towards that silhouette. He walked for a long time, never seeming to get any closer, until almost immediately he was right behind him.

"Hello?" he whispered to the figure. Nothing. "Hello?" he tapped him on the shoulder.

The figure whipped around and he found himself face to face with Cole, who had a maniacal look on his face and was holding a photo. The image burned into Jack's brain, he knew it would come back to haunt him: that naked picture of Charmaine.

"I believe you stole this..." Cole whispered menacingly.

Jack was about to retort the claim but wasn't fast enough, receiving a back hand across the cheek which threw him to the ground, then getting kicked and stomped in the gut and on the chest by Cole. It felt like all his ribs were breaking. The metallic taste of blood filled his mouth. Cole grabbed him by his hair and forcibly dunked his head in the icy water of the lake, repeatedly dunking it in and out and then finally holding his head under the water. Jack could feel his lungs desperate for air. "This is it," he thought, "this is how I go." A noise of distant bells chimed in his head, getting louder and louder as if they were getting closer and closer. Through the icy water he could make out the hands of a clock spinning wildly—nothing was left to control the hands, nothing to slow time's unceasing progression towards death and nothingness. The cold water filled his lungs and everything went black.

"Peter…"

"Peter…"

He could hear his brother's name echoing through the emptiness, what did it mean? Was his brother's name to be the last he ever heard? Was this what Hell was like?

CHAPTER VIII

"I sought to hear the voice of God and climbed the topmost steeple, but God declared: 'Go down again—I dwell among the people.'"

—*John Henry Newman*

"Peter..."

The colour returned as quickly as it had gone and he could see the common room once more, being jolted out of his sleep by the clock chiming eight o'clock. He was sweaty and clammy, but otherwise unscathed.

"Peter..."

It was still Tom nudging him awake, but this time he was pretty sure it was real life.

"Peter..."

"I'm not...I mean, yeah what do you want, Tom?"

"Sorry for waking you."

"What do you want?"

"Come quickly," he said. "All my drawings have disappeared from my room."

"What on Ear…oh, those drawings. Yes." Jack looked puzzled for a little while. "And what do you want me to do about that?"

He looked around the room. Everyone seemed to be present and still asleep or at least dozing where they had fallen the night before…except someone was missing…where was Lorenz? Jack heard footsteps coming up the stairs, and a moment later Lorenz swaggered through the door.

"Mr. Latan would like to see you in his office, Tom," Lorenz smirked. All three boys: Tom, Lorenz, and Jack posing as Peter, walked down the stairs and into the deputy's office.

"Thomas Steerforth. I cannot even begin to explain how disappointed I am in you," were Mr. Latan's first words as Tom sat down in the office. "It is gross inappropriateness to be drawing pictures of another student, especially of the opposite sex, like this." He flicked through the drawings pointedly one at a time.

"And Peter…" he was unaware that he was actually addressing Jack "…you knew about it and chose to do nothing?"

"Yes, sir. Well, I thought it was harmless enough." Jack answered, trying to imagine what Peter would say in a situation like that. Though to be fair, it is probably very similar to what he himself would have answered.

"Boys, let me tell you a story. A few years ago, there was a young girl called Wallis who attended St. Scholastica's. A rather quite good looking young lady, if I might say. She wrote poems. Many, many poems—she was always writing poetry. And then one day, in her absence, her roommate looked through a pile of her poems. They were all about one subject, young Father Culpa. Well, the roommate was aghast and went straight away to tell the headmistress, and rightly so! The last anybody ever saw of Wallis Plinge was of her walking through the gardens that night—a stormy, wet, windy tempestuous night. She was never heard of again."

Jack rolled his eyes. "What a load of rubbish," he thought, but he looked across at Tom who seemed to have been put into a worried state by the (at least Jack thought) obviously fabricated story.

"Anyway," the deputy headmaster continued, "the point is that Mrs. Culpa…I mean, the Headmistress, would not be the least bit amused at this. I think detention is in order for the two of you. Thomas , I do wish you would clean up your act. Grow up a bit and all that."

"Excuse me, sir," Jack looked quizzically. "Did you say *Mrs. Culpa*?"

"Yes, quite a slip of the tongue. I meant to say that you'll be doing detention with Fr. Culpa, this evening, getting the chapel ready for mass tomorrow morning."

Lorenz, who had been sitting there the whole time, let out a little smirk. He was back to his old ways after being scolded by Cole, and his determination to bully Tom into an even more miserable position than he was already in was paying off. As the three boys left the office, Jack had a wicked thought—they all thought he was Peter, he was blameless. So he picked up Lorenz around the waist and thrust him out the first-storey window so that he would never cause Tom problems again. And would you believe it—Mr Latan came out of his office cheering Jack on, and Tom high fived Jack and gave him a hug. The end.

But then he snapped out of his daydream and realised that he could only do the next best thing, so he flipped Lorenz off when his back was turned and they went their separate ways.

"Do you think he'll tell Charmaine?" queried Tom.

"Perhaps. I'm not really sure," Jack answered, still being Peter.

Thomas was uneasy about the notion of Charmaine finding out prematurely. How could she fall in love with him if he didn't have the chance to tell her first?

The rest of the morning was difficult. Tom was obviously upset and contemplative, thinking deeply about his next steps. Jack became Jack again at the next opportunity and just hoped that Thomas didn't mention to the real Peter about the detention that evening, at which point Jack would have to become Peter again. But alas, this book isn't one of mistaken identities and rumbustious hilarity, so we won't dwell on that here.

They sat down for lunch in their usual peer group. Saturday lunch was the lull in food quality for the week because, and this was only a suspicion, money had to be saved for the traditional weekly Sunday hot roast. On Saturdays they were served some mess of sloppy peas and a mystery meat—nobody was really sure what went in to this usual weekend meal, but it was generally assumed to be a mixture of what had been eaten throughout the week, plus whatever was on special at the local supermarket.

Tom sat in his usual silence eating his stew, brooding on the events of earlier that day and the inconvenience of his crush's brothers. Lorenz was quite happy with himself and was even more chatty than usual. He kept referencing Charmaine and Cole as if he was trying to rub something in.

"Ah, lads," the red-haired reverend had snuck up behind them. "I'm shocked, but a couple of you seem to have detention with me tonight. Surely this must be a mistake, am I right?" he said with that beautifully friendly smile. He looked at a clipboard he was holding in his hand. "Tom and Peter?" he confirmed.

Peter looked confused. "Oh, no, Father. That must be a mistake." At which point Jack pressed hard on his foot.

"No, that's right," Jack confirmed. "I'm Peter. I'll be at detention tonight."

"You haven't even been here a week, you two, and one of you is already getting detentions? Not a good start really. But it's okay, detention isn't all that bad. We're going to mop the entire chapel together," he grinned sincerely, as if to say he actually did enjoy mopping.

"What on earth," Peter began to Jack as they left the dining hall together. "How did you get me a detention?"

"Relax, Peter. I'm going to do it for you anyway," Jack answered, trying to avoid the question.

Peter stopped. "Okay, but seriously, Jack. What have you done?"

"Do you promise you won't be mad?"

"No, I'm not going to promise that. What have you done?"

"Well, somehow Lorenz found out about Tom's drawings."

"What? You're an idiot. I trusted you with one small bit of information and you told him just because you have the hots for Charmaine too, and you promised…"

"I know, I know. Look, I'm sorry. I was frustrated at Tom the other day but changed my mind when he tried to help me with the apple to Cole's head, but by then it was too late. But…but I have some information you might be interested in?"

Jack recounted to Peter the story that Mr. Latan had told him, and also how he had accidentally slipped up and called the headmistress "Mrs. Culpa." They had, after all, noticed a ring on Fr. Culpa's finger. Could it be that they were married? But he was a Catholic priest— it couldn't be possible.

Evening rolled around and the two boys met Fr. Culpa in the Chapel promptly at seven o'clock. They were expecting back-breaking work accompanied per- haps by a sermon on what they had done wrong or in what they had failed to do.

"Gentlemen!" The priest hollowed as he entered the chapel. "Good evening".

"Good evening, Father," the two boys echoed.

"Now, we need to get this place ready for the ser- vice tomorrow. So many floorboards." Fr Culpa said nonchalantly, scanning around the chapel as if he hadn't been there before. "So, Jack, or Peter, whoever you say you are, you can start by vacuuming the floor- boards and a little after you start, we'll start mopping behind you. Tom, you can move the bucket around behind me while I do the mopping. Go and fill that bucket up there."

Tom headed off to the scullery to fill up the bucket with hot water.

"Sir, how did you know I was Jack?"

"You think I wouldn't notice that you were in your brother's place?"

"I… I guess I didn't know we looked different at all to other people," Jack stuttered. "And let me get this straight. You're going to do the mopping with us?"

"Well, yes, of course. What good would it do any of us for me to sit back and get you two to do all the work? It's not that hard anyhow, keeps me fit and all that. It's an easy yoke to carry, a light burden to bear."

The job was not nearly half as hard as the boys expected. With Fr. Culpa helping, it was even almost enjoyable. He liked telling jokes: that one about the penguin, and the one about the French café where the guy orders an egg, and the lentil/chickpea one—all of those sorts of jokes. When he thought they were sick of his chit-chatting, around the time that they started polishing the wooden pews, he let them listen to the radio, but only to CatholicFM, naturally. They were all done and dusted (if you'll excuse the pun) at half past eight.

"Isn't it amazing," the Father began, "that no matter how dirty something gets, you can always clean it right back up again? It just takes a bit of willpower to recognise the dirt sometimes."

"And you're not mad at us, Father?" Jack asked. "Mr Latan was furious."

"Well, Jack, I find it best to seek to understand, not to accuse. Remember when you talk to Mr. Latan you're talking to someone who thinks Sherlock Holmes is a real estate agency."

Jack laughed, "Perhaps we should get detention more often."

The boys started on their way back to their rooms, relieved that detention hadn't been the horrific circumstance that they thought it would be.

"I can't believe he was so happy to help," Jack began. "What a nice guy."

"I wouldn't be so sure," Tom retorted. "James told me that he heard Fr. Culpa had been in prison before he started working here."

Jack laughed, which wasn't the response Tom thought that comment would get. "Oh, you guys are so gullible. You'd believe anything!"

So they wandered up to their respective rooms and all was well that night.

CHAPTER IX

"We can easily forgive a child who is afraid of the dark;
the real tragedy of life is when men are afraid of the light."

—*Plato*

A s is always the case, the rest of Sunday after church rushed by in no time at all. I really do think there is some conspiracy of time to make the weekends only a small fraction as long as a single weekday. The twins could hardly believe it, but it was already Monday again, and this meant literature just before dinner. The boys sat through the class which was as boring as ever, so dry and insipid that their distraction led to Jack beginning to tell Peter in hushed whispers about Tom's comment about prison the night before.

Mrs Bowen looked up from the copy of the Fitzgerald book she'd been reading from and glared at Jack over the top of her round spectacles.

"Peter. Jack. If you cannot control your urge to whisper sweet nothings between yourselves then you'll need to separate."

A slight muffled giggle passed around the room at this inference.

"Please, Miss, we're listening." Jack said with a face as if he had just been gravely insulted. "We were just discussing that book you're reading."

"Very well, so you would know the main character's mother's name?" The literature teacher asked with a smirk.

Jack turned to Peter, who mouthed a word to him.

Jack swivelled confidently back to the teacher. "Butress," he answered with bravado. "Also known as, I believe, Mrs. Carraway…she lives in the South of France and has to go to a psychiatric hospital in Switzerland…I think." He continued, getting more and more unsure as he went. Meanwhile, Peter had put his head in his hands in despair.

Ms Bowen separated them on the grounds that Jack obviously had no idea what was going on. She had been reading *This Side of Paradise* and Jack clearly had not been listening.

So they resorted to what any pairs of adolescents would do when separated part way through a conversation—pass notes between themselves, the first of which caught the eye of Mrs. Bowen. Of course, the note ended up with the teacher, who read it and quickly told them to see her after class.

"Fr Culpa has been in jail before," she read out to the two boys now standing before her at the front of the empty classroom. "Now, why would two boys such as yourselves be talking about this?" she asked.

"Please, Miss, is it true?" Peter responded.

The old lady sighed. "I've known Fr Culpa since he was your age," she reminisced. "I will tell you, but only to clear up any misinformation you might've heard so that you don't get the wrong idea of him. I hear you've been writing down secrets, would you like to write mine down?"

The twins agreed. They couldn't pass up an opportunity like this, especially a secret belonging to someone that would probably die soon.

"SECRET OF MS. T. BOWEN –
COLLECTED ON MONDAY 13/05/2019
@ ST. BENEDICT'S COLLEGE.

'This all happened twelve years ago, but it haunts my mind to this very day. I owned a pawn shop that specialised in antiques on a windy little lane in the middle of the city. I had bought the small shop from an elderly couple who had owned it their whole life as a florist, but had decided to retire and sell the shop. I moved into the apartment above the shop—it was my whole life. I had had a fascination with antiques and old items since I was a young girl and decided to follow my dreams, even though I knew the risks and the low success rates of those sorts of businesses.

I started the shop with a small collection of items. Business was slow but every couple of days someone would come in and meander through the collection. We occasionally had a sale, but nowhere near enough to keep me afloat. I took out loan after loan from the bank until my apartment and the shop was in danger of repossession. I tried so many different methods to arouse interest in my little shop: signs, handing out flyers, newspaper ads. Nothing seemed to increase business noticeably. I was desperate, my life was falling apart around me.

Then one night I was watching a documentary about the famous seventeenth century musical instrument maker Stradivarius. They estimated that he made 2000 instruments and only about 650 were accounted for. Well, I had a couple of old violins in my shop, so I decided to go down and have a check to see if there might be a label on them. Alas, none of them had the label, but I had a wicked thought, born out of desperation. I knew enough about what the label would look like to write one to imitate a Stradivarius. I had studied calligraphy in my youth, so how hard could it be? I confided in a close friend of mine, Mr. Manea, who was an antique appraiser. We agreed to be in it together, splitting the money equally.

The next day, an old gentleman came in and was looking around when I casually mentioned one of the violins in the shop was very old. He looked it over and noticed the label, asking where and when I had gotten the violin. I claimed to have not known, but pointed out that it had all the hallmarks of being an actual Strad. He asked what the monetary worth of it might be, and I answered that it would be in the region of a couple of million.

Well, he took it to Manea's workshop and got it appraised for much more than it was worth, and returned later in the day to buy it. This faded old instrument that was worth no more than any other counterfeit was sold for two million. My quaint shop was now on the map and news reporters came flocking. I was interviewed for the paper and I guess it gave me a big head. Business boomed as more and more of these 'extremely valuable' items flowed out of the shop, nobody ever suspecting our counterfeiting. Clocks, furniture, books, music…we sold everything at an inflated price with fake labels. We were cunning in our business, extorting but taking care not to arise suspicion. It was meant to end after the first sale, which would have been enough to save my store. But I had the taste of money and of success, so I kept the scam going. That's the problem with lying – once you start, it becomes harder and harder to stop.

Business was so strong that I had to hire an assistant. I put a poster up and an enthusiastic fourteen-year-old boy with bright red hair came enquiring. This was perfect I thought—a young boy would never suspect anything and would be perfect for the job. He did the job very well, keeping the shop clean and tidy, organising the items, and never suspecting that anything out of the ordinary might be going on directly under his nose. He was the perfect assistant—polite, attentive, proactive. Little did I know that when he grew up he would become a very close friend of mine. Young Felix added some much-needed youthful energy to my shop.

This went on for about six months, until one fateful night that would change my life. It was a dark and cold night. An icy wind whipped through the alleyway and the snow pelted down, almost a blizzard. We were just closing up, young Felix was sweeping the showroom floor while I balanced the books for the day. Suddenly the door swung open, pushed by the snow and the wind, and an old woman hobbled in on her walking stick, carrying a large and heavy book in the other hand. She was wearing a thick fur cashmere and was rugged up from headscarf to black buckled shoes with layer upon layer.

I was already around seventy at the time, but she likely would have been over a hundred. Felix ran to close the door behind her and offered to carry the book to the counter for her, but she said she was okay carrying the burden herself. She continued hobbling to the counter where she laid down the book.

"Tomorrow will be a fortnight since my husband died and I need to sell this to continue to put food on my table. How much do you think it might be worth?" she asked in her croaky old voice.

I offered my condolences and then quickly leafed through the stocky book. It was a very old bible, possibly late seventeenth century.

It would be worth a few hundred dollars probably, but then a thought popped into my head. I had heard, only in passing, of a special bible. A mythical bible, in which the printing press had jammed at the point of writing Isaiah 14:12 and had written the word 'devil' backwards. The story goes that the devil himself had caused the jam, and that the press in question had to be sanctified until it would work again. I thought, on the off chance, I may as well check, so flicked to Isaiah

14:12, pretending to just be casually picking a random page to look at.

And this is what I read: 'How you have fallen from heaven, O liveD, morning star, son of the dawn! You have been cast down to the earth, you who once laid low the nations!'

That's right. It should have read 'O Devil,' and yet here I was staring at the reverse. I kept my cool.

"Oh, I would say it's worth about a hundred dollars," I earnestly told the frail woman. "It's a nice edition, but nothing special—there are a lot of these older bibles around."

"Oh, are you sure? I thought it might be worth a little bit more. Please, I need the money."

"Okay, for you, I'll go to one hundred and ten dollars, but I just can't go any higher. I'm sorry."

She stood up and suddenly sneered. "You snake, I know what this is. I know you flipped to Isaiah 14:12. I know the true value of this bible. All of this," she motioned around the shop "all of this is fake. I've been watching and I know they're all counterfeits. I'm going straight to the authorities."

She tried to grab the bible off the table, but I too went to grab it. We both had our hands on it, and she started screeching, ordering me to let it go. Felix stood their broom in hand, dumbfounded over two elderly women playing tug-of-war over a book. I ordered him to come and help me grab it off her but he was frozen in place.

And then a truly horrible thought entered my mind, the worst I had ever had. She was pulling the book with all her weight. So I let go. She went tumbling backwards, hitting her head on the cold hard ground, cracking her fragile skull open in a fresh pool of blood, dead upon impact. Felix was horrified so I sent him home while I cleaned up, then went to his house later to sit him down and explain everything that had happened, making him promise to never tell a single soul. He agreed, but…"

Here, the confession abruptly stops. From what I can tell, Adam burst into the room at this exact moment and told Ms. Bowen and the twins that something big was happening in the dining hall. The twins rushed to the dining hall to find that dinner had finished but that there were still around thirty students there sitting in dribs and drabs, having been stopped in their post-dinner conversations by Thomas who was now standing up at the front of the dining hall addressing the remaining students.

"And this…" flicking his finger across his tablet to show a photo "…is Cole sitting with this girl late at night on the bench out the front of college."

It seemed that Tom had begun an impromptu presentation of his evidence of Cole cheating on

Charmaine. Cole and Charmaine were sitting together, remaining surprisingly calm, while Lorenz sat at table number eight with his mouth agape in pure shock and horror of what was happening.

"As you can see," Tom's voice began to falter as he realised that this was no longer a scene conjured up in his imagination, that this was real. "Cole is seeing this dark-haired girl in secret. And who knows how many other girls…and…and boys…and other things…he is seeing at the moment to satisfy himself. Charmaine, you don't need to put up with this. You're too good for him. I would treat you so much better. I can give you the world if you'll let me. We could be…" He trailed off as he realised that Cole had stood up and was walking calmly towards him.

"Thank you, Thomas, for that presentation. But even through your disturbing tendency to stalk me, you seemed to have missed one crucial fact. Do you know what that is, Steerforth?"

Tom slowly shook his head, a sense of dread came over him.

"The fact that I have a sister, Ebony. Who coincidentally is identical to all those pictures you showed us. But it's okay, you were just looking out for Charmaine, so I forgive you."

He was now next to Tom, and he put his arm round and patted Tom on the back, pretending to be civil and calm, cradling Tom around the shoulder.

"Just make sure it doesn't happen again, hey old sport? We wouldn't want another *misunderstanding*." With that, he punched Tom square in the gut, forcing him to wince and shrink to the ground while holding his stomach in pain.

"Leave him alone!" Peter yelled from the other side of the dining hall. He raced up to where Cole was standing and all of a sudden the hall went into that frenzied pubescent bloodlust call of "Fight! Fight! Fight!" But Peter was smarter than that and knew he couldn't take on Cole, so he brushed past him and went straight to Tom who was now lying on the floor, both hands on his gut as if putting pressure on a gunshot wound.

"Lorenz!" Cole shouted. "Bring me his bag. Let's see what other stalking the little creep's been doing."

Lorenz obeyed, grabbing Tom's bag from under the table and running up to the front where Cole was standing. He emptied the contents onto the floor in a symbolic action of dominance. Everything fell out, mostly school books and papers and stationery. But then, after all this had tumbled to the ground, a single photo floated down. Lorenz picked it up, staring at it once again in shock, the colour draining from his face.

"Where…how…?"

"What is it?" Cole asked.

Lorenz continued to stand there as if he had seen a ghost.

"What is it?" Cole repeated, snatching it off him and having a look for himself.

Cole started shaking with rage. It was, of course, the picture Jack had stuffed in a bag under the table in his panic a few days ago, unaware that it was Tom's bag. The scuffle that broke out as a result of this picture was loud and unruly. Cole went straight for the already doubled-over Tom with a look of manic anger in his eyes. Peter tried to hold him off but it was no use. Cole was just too big. Jack and Lorenz also joined in on either side of the chaos, the result being a mess of punches, kicks, and grappling until the two sides separated on the intervention of Mr. Latan.

"Everybody, go to your rooms immediately. This behaviour is not acceptable. We will get to the root of this problem one person at a time."

"Can I go with Tom, Sir?" Peter asked.

"May. And no, you may not. I said everybody to their own rooms, you are no exception, Mr. Lapin."

But Fr. Culpa was standing behind him, and gave a little nod of acceptance. "Thank you," Peter mouthed to the Priest.

Peter went with Tom, and Jack dallied on his way to an inevitably long and awkward time with Cole. Jack had a momentous decision to make—to confess to the origins of the photo and risk himself, or to leave it be and escape consequence?

Jack eventually got to his room, finding Cole sitting on his bed with fists clenched, not even greeting him as he entered. Jack sat on his bed, opposite Cole, and remained speechless for a while. You could feel the suffocating tension in the air between them.

"So…" Jack began, "that was interesting?"

"Shut up," Cole snapped.

"Well, okay. I'd just like to say that I had nothing to do with this though. You can't blame me, mate."

Still silence.

"I don't approve of what Tom did, but he's young and stupid. Don't be too angry at him."

Finally Cole spoke, his head falling down to his cupped hands, on the verge of tears.

"Don't be too angry? How can I not be angry? First he accuses me of cheating on Charmaine, then I find a naked picture of her in his bag? I try to be a good person, and I try not to bully him, but then he does stupid things like this. What am I supposed to do, look the other way and pretend that he's not perving on my girlfriend and stealing from me? Some people make themselves impossible to like. Tom just stumbles around in ignorance and stupidity until people have no choice but to bully him."

Jack sat their perplexed. Who was this person that sat on the bed across from him? It dawned on Jack that he knew almost nothing about Cole and had never bothered to ask. Perhaps he was human after all? "I don't know, talk to him about it maybe? Try to forgive him?" was all he could muster.

"We're beyond talking about it. He needs to learn that he can't do things like that. He has to pay."

Meanwhile, Peter had a tough time comforting Tom who was inconsolable. He had not fared well in his battle against the much larger and formidable Cole. Nothing seemed broken but he was a bit battered and bruised, his nose had stopped bleeding but his shirt was stained with drops of blood.

"Do you think Charmaine thought I was brave?" Tom finally squeaked.

"Maybe, Tom, or maybe she just thought you were stupid. But maybe bravery and stupidity are the same thing a lot of the time. Now, let's get you cleaned up, hey?" Peter said, helping him to stand up. His legs were weak and he needed the support of Peter even to hold him up, but with the older boy's help, he managed to get changed into clean clothes and clean his blood-ied-up face.

Mr. Latan decided to leave the resolving of issues until the morning as it was getting late. Things did seem, however, to be heading in the right direction. Perhaps the events that had led to the heated scuffle would now be resolved. As Jack's eyes became heavy, he recited in his head what he was going to say to

Cole the next day to confess and apologise deeply. He hoped that Cole would understand and that all could turn over a new leaf.

The lights went out at their usual time and, to the birds flying high above the colleges, nothing would have seemed out of the ordinary. In fact, it probably seemed calmer and quieter than usual. The night rolled on, and as the moon rose higher in the cloudless sky, a figure trudged through the glistening blades of grass towards the front doors of the college—a silent stranger wandering through the emptiness of night. Nobody woke up to hear him. They all lied in undisturbed sleep tucked up in their comfortable beds with their soft blankets, all except for Thomas Steerforth who was already lying at the bottom of the college pool, motionless and lifeless, his left foot chained and locked to a dumbbell, his lungs full of water. A place where his downtrodden heart could pine for Charmaine no longer.

CHAPTER X

"To die, to sleep—
To sleep, perchance to dream—ay, there's the rub,
For in this sleep of death what dreams may come..."

—*William Shakespeare, Hamlet*

Tom's body was found early the next morning when a group of boys went down to the pool for their morning fitness. Upon diving in to start his laps, the first boy quickly resurfaced frantically babbling and pointing to the spot where he had seen Tom's naked body chained to the dumbbell. It was understandably quite a shock to him.

Needless to say, the pool was closed for the rest of the day and the police were called. The school was put into complete lockdown which meant that the boys had to stay in their rooms, no classes were held that day, and meals were taken in complete silence in the dining hall as the grave discomfort loomed over the entire school. Mr. Latan ran around like a headless chicken, trying to assure staff and students alike that everything was alright. The students had their doubts, and the wiser among them started to think that Mr. Latan's head may be on the chopping block if any negligence was found.

Peter and Jack were, of course, upset beyond words upon hearing the news. Peter sat in his room sobbing for most of the day, while Jeremy Fisher did all that he could to comfort him. Jack also sat sobbing in his room, but received no such comfort from Cole who sat playing on his phone for most of the day, ignoring Jack's muffled cries. Teachers came by periodically to check up on the students and to comfort those who were distressed.

Ding! Cole's game had advanced a level.

"Don't you even care?" squinted Jack. "Don't you even care that someone you know has died suddenly and tragically?"

"Of course I care, but there's no point crying over it is there? That won't do anything."

Jack couldn't bring himself to continue the conversation, considering that he deeply suspected in his mind that Cole had either murdered Tom or had at least been instrumental in his death. They didn't talk for the rest of the day, there was no point. If Cole didn't understand the gravitas of the situation then there was nothing Jack could do to help him.

Tom's body had been taken for investigation and all the relevant bureaucracy had been covered. The investigation and autopsy would most likely take a couple of weeks, after which action could be taken depending on what was discovered. Tom's foster parents had been informed and his foster mum came down to the school to travel with the body to the morgue. His dad was busy working that day. Tom's room was to be left alone until a time when it could be investigated thoroughly for clues as to why he might have drowned himself.

After dinner, Jack snuck out and joined Peter in his room. Finally being away from Cole felt like the greatest relief Jack had ever experienced in his life, and it was the first time he had been able to speak to Peter alone since hearing of the incident. He wrapped his arms around Peter in a hug and they softly sobbed together. After minutes passed this way, they sat together on his bed.

"I…I just can't believe it," Peter stammered. "How could this happen?"

"I know," Jack said as he wiped the tears from his own eyes. "It's just horrible".

They sat silently for a few good minutes until Peter started talking again.

"What do you think happened?" He asked. "Has Cole said anything?"

"No, Cole doesn't seem to care too much about it all. He's been playing games on his phone all day. I'm not sure what part Cole played in it—he was there when I fell asleep and then I didn't wake up until this morning, and he was still there."

"...and Lorenz?" asked Peter.

"Again, I'm not sure. I haven't spoken to him all day. Couldn't bring myself to start a discussion with him at lunch or dinner. He seemed really out of it. Didn't seem to acknowledge anyone around him. Other than that, I don't know how he's been taking it. I assume he'll be..." but Jack trailed off when he noticed that Peter wasn't really listening anymore. He had stood up while Jack was talking and was now intently watching out the window with a bewildered look on his face.

"That looks like..." Peter started, but Jack immediately stood up to see what his twin was looking at. "That looks like Lorenz sitting on the bench out there. And look. Fr Culpa is walking towards him."

The boys were correct. Under that famous lone apple tree sat Lorenz, staring out into the forest. The forest that had once looked so full of wonder to him—sparkling with damp leaves that glistened in the beauty of the moonlight now took on a different appearance. A place that, for the last few years, had provided a feeling of shelter and solitude now looked like a dark, uninviting wasteland. The sun had just finished setting and the splayed colours of sunset were quickly fading into a dark, moonless night. The forest looked frightening to him now, a dark bastion that had become devoid of all meaning. The dry dead leaves clung mercilessly to their branches as the cold wind blew its accidental course through the grotesque, inconsequential trees. As he stared, he started to hear footsteps behind him coming closer and closer. Lorenz turned slowly, half expecting to see Cole approaching him.

"Father?" he squinted confusedly. "Why are you here?"

"Well, Lorenz, I could see you from my rectory window and thought that you might need someone to talk to. How are you doing? Why are you out here?"

"Well...I don't know Father. I guess maybe I'm just feeling a bit lost."

"Well, I happen to think we're all a bit lost sometimes," the priest smiled. "It's whether we become found again that's most important."

Peter and Jack couldn't possibly hear what they were saying from such a great distance, but they could make them out as having a conversation together on that bench underneath the apple tree.

"What do you think they're saying?" asked Jack. "Do you think...no, it couldn't be."

"Do I think what?"

Jack thought for a moment how to approach the complicated subject. "Well, Fr Culpa must have so many things to do right now, and yet he's taking the time to sit out there with Lorenz and have a long conversation. How does he have time for that? It must be pretty important."

"Go on...?" enquired Peter.

"Well, all I'm saying is, don't you think it's strange that Fr Culpa played a part in all the secrets that we heard? He covered up for Bowen when she killed that old lady. He saw that girl Wallis in his room the night she disappeared. He took a particular interest in Tom, even going so far as getting him a place in the school. He acts like such a nice guy but we know his dark history. Do you think he and Lorenz had something to do with Tom's death?"

"Jack, are you suggesting that Fr Culpa might have killed Tom or got Lorenz to do it?"

"Well, I mean, it's not as far-fetched as it sounds. He's nice...too nice. And I doubt whether he's even a priest at all. We both know he's married to the headmistress. Her name's Mrs. Culpa, it's like they didn't even try to keep it a secret."

"But why would he murder Tom?"

"Perhaps he knew too much, perhaps he and the reverend were a little too close, if you know what I mean. Perhaps he's a psychopath who gets off on mur-dering people? What if we're next?"

Peter and Jack both thought on this. It *did* seem strange that the priest had appeared to be involved in so many incidences, and that out of all the things he could be doing to improve the situation, he was now sitting alone with Lorenz speaking in hushed whispers. What secrets were they exchanging, the twins wondered?

"I think we need to confront Fr Culpa once he fin-ishes with Lorenz." Peter decided.

So the twins waited, completely unaware of the content of the conversation that went on below them. The young man and the boy conversed for about an hour before the older one stood up, patted Lorenz on the back, and walked back through the glistening blades of grass towards the rectory. The twins had decided that they needed to know the truth. They were going to talk to Fr Culpa and then to Lorenz, cross-ref-erence the story, and then go talk to Cole, all in an effort to try and solve the riddle of Tom's death.

Death is a fascinating phenomenon. A great author once described the feeling of losing a loved one as that of walking up a familiar set of stairs but thinking that there was one more step than there really was. It can bring out the best in people—where would David have ended up without Uriah? What would have become of Scrooge if Marley had not died? What would the world be like had

Christ not been crucified? But alas, here we are not talking about a martyr, or a literary figure, or God incarnate. No, here we must discuss the death of a thirteen-year-old boy with hair as innocently blond as a chick, and with intentions as pure as the moonlight itself. A true tragedy. He never came to know his parents—the truth being that they had never wanted a child and that they were never coming back to find him like they do in all of those happy *"histoires d'orphelins."* I truly hate to say it, but if you were expecting an "Oliver" or "Annie" ending, then you might be disappointed. Just like in life, not all stories end happily, and the vast multitude of deaths in the real world are not kind or symbolic or life-changing. But that is the way of the world. Death is an inevitable part of life.

The moon didn't rise that night. It must have been with the sun, inhabiting the day time on the other face of the earth. It was particularly dark as Peter and Jack made their way across the damp, cold grass towards the rectory. Once they arrived, they knocked on the door three times and waited to confront their priest to get the story straight. All the while, the birds that always seemed to circle the college had landed for the night, nesting on the rusted gutters and creaky roof tiles of St. Benedict's. For once they were not squawking, but rather watching in silent omniscience as the priest opened the door and welcomed the twins into a warm and hospitable reception room.

CHAPTER XI

"You are not what others think you are.
You are what God knows you are."

—*Shannon Alder*

"**A**h, Peter, Jack! I wasn't expect…"

"We know, Father." Peter interjected.

"Well, have a seat, lads. What brings you here? I expect you're both extremely upset?"

"We're devastated," Jack said coldly, trying not to give anything away.

"As am I, boys, as am I. Such a tragedy. He was far too young."

"Are you really, Father?" Peter said cynically.

"What do you mean? Of course, I'm devastated by this. Why would you think I'm not?"

Peter decided to take the lead in explaining themselves. "We saw you talking to Lorenz just now. Strange person to be having a long conversation with given what's just happened. And we've heard a lot of things about you which we find very questionable."

"Oh…I see. Well, what sort of things have you heard about me that would make you question my character?" The priest asked defensively.

"I don't even know where to start. You seem very married considering you claim to be a Catholic priest. I assume you just got this farce-of-a-job from your wife who runs the whole show. And we know that when you were fourteen you witnessed an elderly lady being murdered and helped to cover up for the person who…coincidentally…is now the English teacher at this school and a close friend of yours? Does the name Wallis Plinge ring a bell? And then…we know you're experienced at sneaking around behind the scenes. Somehow you managed to convince Thomas' parents out of a fortune so that he could come here. So I guess the game's up. Who are you really? Tom's father? Ms Bowen's young lover? Or just a murderer?"

As Peter finished, he was surprised at what had just come out of his mouth. There was no going back from there. Even Jack was a little irked. Were they really accusing the effervescent red-haired man in front of them of all of this?

"Well, I'm afraid to say you've got it all wrong, Peter." The priest said after a thoughtful pause. "But I understand that you're upset and I'm not angry at you for bringing all of this up. I am a little disappointed in you though, I never would have expected you to come to those conclusions."

"Okay, then. If you can explain it then we'll listen," Peter had realised how manic his accusations had sounded and was looking for a chance to back out of the hole he had dug himself into.

"Well, where do I start? Do you want to write it down like you have the other secrets you've been keeping? Though none of it's a secret, all you had to do was ask and I would have told you. Please, sit down," he ushered to the boys to sit on the seat opposite him. They only just realised that they had been standing the whole time, so wound up in their accusations and exasperated emotional state.

"The headmistress, Mia Culpa, is my sister, not my wife. I was once engaged to be married, but it was not to be. In fact, my life was quite different only a few years ago from what it is now and I probably have to tell you a lot about it so that you can understand. When I was fourteen, I did indeed become an assistant shopkeeper to Ms Bowen. And one night I did witness an old lady die because of the greed and avarice of my employer. I was told never to tell anyone and I never did. But I don't think you heard the end of that story. The morning after that fateful night, I went back to the shop and spoke with Ms Bowen. I told her that the right thing to do would be for her to turn herself in. Deep down, she knew that, and I think she knew that if she didn't confess, then the investigation would find it out anyway, whether through me or just through circumstantial evidence. So she turned herself in and was only charged with manslaughter, as she hadn't meant to kill the old lady. She went to jail for many years. The scandal was splashed all over the newspapers and she and Mr. Manea lost their reputations as trustworthy antique dealers and appraisers.

In the meantime, I kept up with my schooling, and in my senior year was Head Boy and dux of the school. So, of course, I chose my path based on what was expected of me. I decided to study a double of geology and engineering at the most prestigious university in the country. And I did well. I moved on to masters, fell in love with a girl in my class, and graduated with first class honours. I got a high paying job as a geotechnical engineer, bought a house, and became engaged to the woman of my dreams. But a couple of months into our engagement, she got a letter from the Paris Dance Conservatoire, offering her a place in one of the most envied courses in the world. Dancing had always been her passion, so she sat down with me and told me that she couldn't pass up the opportunity, and that it meant our relationship wouldn't work. She gave me the ring back and I never heard from her or saw her again.

Well, I was upset of course, and started feeling bitter from being rejected and unloved. I felt that I could forge my destiny by living for myself, that I could prove to her and to everyone that she had made the wrong decision. That I could be a successful and happy person if I made a good wage, bought a grandiose house and impress an even more beautiful wife into my life. That was alright for a while. I buried myself in work, and I did make a lot of money, but I started wondering what the goal was—where did this all end? What was I going to do with my money? I started finding little ways to try and make more: gambling online, going to the casino, overcharging clients slightly, working weekends. Anything to make an extra dime. But in this cold and heartless pursuit I found myself wanting more, and more, and more still. Becoming sadder with every dollar in my account, greedier with every paycheque.

Then one day everything changed. I went to do a consultation with a client at their home in High Wycombe, only about half an hour from my townhouse in Oxford. There had been a fault found in the way the foundation of the house had been poured, so

I was contracted to survey the block of land and the foundations. I went, but it would probably be about a three month job so I decided it would be good to get to know the family a bit. Their names were Bill and Nancy, and they had a dog called Bullseye, and a five-year-old blond boy named Thomas. Over the months, I came to find out that he wasn't their biological son, that he was a foster kid, and that Bill and Nancy's marriage was rocky because Nancy had found and fell in love with a man twenty years her junior. The project ended up getting cancelled because of the messy divorce and the eventual demolition of the house. The last I heard from them was that Thomas would have to move to another foster home. Nancy met me alone at a café one afternoon, not wanting Bill or Thomas to be there. She asked me if I might be willing to foster Tom, as otherwise he would have to go to some unknown new couple and he was already in a fragile state from problems he had encountered earlier in his childhood. She said that Tom had grown attached to me, and upon watching me do my job, had said that he wanted to become an engineer. That over the last few months, I had become a role model and almost a father-figure to him. Well, it was sad but I really thought nothing of it: just business as usual. Of course it was a no from me. Not my problem.

That summer, I started going to church again on an invitation from a friend that I had met while studying for my masters. I had stopped going during my university years. You know, too busy for Sunday mornings. And there, in the lofty yet cosy chapel of Oxford's Trinity College, where I had studied, God found me. During those sermons about love and compassion, I started thinking about Tom again and how I could have changed his life. As Napoleon said, "The world suffers a lot not because of the violence of bad people, but because of the silence of good people." I started to wonder where he might have turned up and whether he was alright. I tried to investigate what had happened to him, but the department couldn't help me much due to privacy concerns, so there was really nothing I could do. I left no stone unturned in my quest to find out what had become of him, but it yielded only dead ends.

I had a week of leave accrued from work and Mia had just become the headmistress of St. Scholastica's, so I decided I would go visit her and spend the week with her. Well, it is a beautiful school, but when I got here I could hardly believe the differences between St. Scholastica's and St. Benedict's. I saw my own reflection in how she ran the school: obsessed with money, trying to cut corners to put more coins in the coffers, completely neglecting St. Benedict's so that St.

Scholastica's could flourish. I saw that what she was doing was wrong and unjust, and that what I had been doing in my business ventures were the same. It was on the train ride home from seeing Mia that I decided I wasn't happy with how I was living my life. So I changed it. It was like falling in love all over again: it happened little by little, and then suddenly all at once. I quit my job, joined the seminary, and became a priest. I then convinced Mia that the boys at St. Benedict's needed a chaplain, and that I would do it without pay so long as my living needs could be met. She reluctantly agreed and so I started working here.

A few years later, well, you wouldn't believe it. Who walks into my chapel but little Thomas Steerforth? A bit older and a bit bigger but definitely the same boy I that had attached himself to me all those years ago. He didn't remember me from my days as an engineer, but I couldn't forget that face. I had morning tea with him, and he told me all about his life. About how he wasn't happy and that he felt unwanted in his current foster home. So with the money that I had saved up during my working days, I made an offer to his parents. I would pay for his entire education, they didn't have to lift a finger. Mia thought this was foolish. 'Why pay for one orphan underling if you can't pay for them all. It's pointless,' she would say. But I tried, and continue to try, to change her way of thinking. Tom never knew that I was paying for him, but that was part of the joy of it—to be a light in the world without casting a shadow. To not let your right hand know what your left is doing.

About a year after I began teaching here, Ms. Bowen's time in prison finished and she was left released with her old life in ruins, she needed a fresh start. The college was looking for a literature teacher and I encouraged her to apply, a job she was more than aptly qualified for. She had changed, the greed and avarice that had clouded her vision during that time at the shop had gone and she was content living out the rest of her life as a literature teacher here.

As for Wallis Plinge…well, she was a troubled young lady. She would come and talk to me most nights about her issues. It was decided that she should leave the school, as we found out she had an unhealthy obsession with me. If I were you, I wouldn't take much notice of Mr Latan's stories—they're just designed to scare you.

As for speaking to Lorenz just now…well, that's my job. Although he may not show it, he's a very insecure young man. He doesn't fit in and has never really had a role model. His father sent him here when he was very young, he hardly knew a word of English. He used to sit with me right on that chair that you're sitting on and we would go through his homework word by word. I spent many hours in this room with him explaining grammar, language, even life in general. And now look at his English—almost native-level apart from his infamous jumbling of idioms." The priest let out a little sigh of laughter. "I think most of all he was glad to meet someone who could speak French with him as well as I could. He always has, and still does, struggle with relating to people, so he acts up and takes it out on others. He's not a bad kid, he's just lost and confused."

Peter squirmed uncomfortably in his seat. How could they have been so wrong? How could their judge of character of this man have been so far off the truth? Death can make even the most logical of us act unexplainably illogical. But what of Lorenz?

"So," Peter began, "what were you talking to Lorenz about earlier this evening?"

"Peter, I can't tell you that. What students tell me in confidence I cannot repeat to other students. If I were you, I would stay out of the whole affair. Nothing good will come of it."

"Yes, Father, we will," Jack answered.

Upon that final promise, the twins bade farewell to the priest and went to start on their way back to their rooms. It was as black as coal outside now. The moon would be absent all night, the sky looked like a raven's feather. The boys walked and talked, and talked and walked. Fr Culpa's story seemed true, but they were filled with curiosity. It had shed a lot of light on his life, but had not done anything to explain Tom's death.

So they hatched a plan. Lorenz had always taken more of a shining to Jack than he had to Peter, so Jack would go and talk to him. Peter, meanwhile, would go and try and get some information from Cole, as Jack couldn't even bear the thought of going and spending time with Cole again. So they climbed those stairs that they had ascended so many times and remembered the first time they had climbed them, the memory of Tom carrying their cases in front of them now seemed like a perverse miscarriage of justice. What had seemed like a day full of opportunity and the promise of a new life now seemed like the start of a dark spiral of death. At the top of the staircase, they went their separate ways, Peter heading to Cole's room and Jack going straight to find Lorenz. Little did they know it would be the last time they climbed those stairs together.

CHAPTER XII

"One of the greatest tragedies in life is to lose
your own sense of self and accept the version
of you that is expected by everyone else."

—*K.L. Toth*

Jack found Lorenz in his room. He was sitting on
his bed just blankly staring forward. He didn't
even notice Jack knock on the open door the first
time, but quickly whipped around in a fright the second time that Jack knocked.

"Lorenz," Jack pleaded as he invited himself in, "if
you know anything about Tom's death, and I suspect
you do, then you need to tell me about it."

"I, well, I…"

"Please, Lorenz, I can help you if you tell me what
happened."

"Okay…but will you do something for me?"

"Anything, Lorenz. Anything."

"Will you sleep in my room tonight? That bed is spare." He pointed across the room. "I'm scared, I don't want to be alone."

"Okay, yes, I guess I can do that. Why are you scared?"

"I told Fr. Culpa everything and the police are probably on their way now, as we speak. And if Cole finds out and comes and finds me, he'll kill me. I need someone here to protect me."

"Okay, Lorenz. I'll stay. Why would Cole want to kill you? What did you see last night?"

"I hit the bag early and went to bed before lights out," he started. "I was still a bit shaken by what had happened in the dining hall and I had the trouble falling to sleep. But then just before midnight, I was shook awake by this big shadow of a man. At first I thought I was dreaming, but it turned out to be Cole. I asked him what he was doing and he told me to get up, get dressed, and come with him. He said he wanted to sneak Tom out and talk to him, perhaps rough him up a little. So in my half asleep state I agreed, and went and woke Tom up softly, telling him what Cole had told me to. 'Charmaine wants to talk to you,' I said. James briefly woke up and sleepily asked what we were doing, so I told him we were just going for a walk and that we'd be back soon. Tom got dressed and wiped the sleep from his eyes, walked along with me. He seemed pretty excited, I guess he thought that Charmaine had been impressed with his exposé. Well, we went down the stairs and out a side door where we knew no one would be watching. And I…"

Lorenz was starting to get teary again, as he let out a deep sigh.

"I led him right out the door that Cole was waiting next to, and he pounced and grabbed Tom, lifting him right off the ground. He covered his mouth with one hand and hoisted him up under the armpits with the other. I had gotten him ambushed. I followed them into the forest and Cole took a role of gaffer tape out of his pocket to cover Tom's mouth with it. He screamed, but it was muffled so much by the tape that it could hardly be heard. We started heading towards the lake, all the while Cole held Tom's hands behind his back, pushing him along as he stumbled over the tree roots and uneven ground. I followed silently, trying to figure out what Cole had in store for him. We were getting near the lake now, and then we stopped. Cole pulled Tom's shirt off over his head, undid Tom's belt, and slid his shorts to the ground. It looked like we were going to the lake to dunk him in. And then he turned to me. 'Take your shirt off, Lorenz,' he ordered. 'But it's cold out here,' I said. He told me just to do it, so I did it. Then he told me to take my shorts off too. 'If we're dunking him in the lake, I'm not going in to. It's too cold,' I said. He just rolled his eyes and then whisked Tom away again, this time heading deeper into the forest. We stopped again. 'Take your shorts off,' he repeated to me, 'or I'll take them off for you.' I could hear the agitation in his voice, he was losing it. He was actually turning insane right in front of me, turning into an animal. So I reluctantly took them off, and there we were, two young boys standing in their underwear on a cold, dark night, a much larger figure looming over the both of us. I asked what we were going to do to him and he told me that if Tom liked Charmaine so much, he would have to settle for her brother. I looked at him in confusion. 'What do you mean?' I questioned."

Lorenz told Jack exactly what Cole had in mind, though I feel that this is not the place to write it. We will maintain the decorum of this retelling of events and just say that it was something that disgusted Lorenz, and something that he would never willingly do. But he was afraid and Cole was a formidable force.

"My heart started pounding, I could hear it beating in my head and feel it in my neck. Cole put his hands down the front of Tom's underwear and..." Lorenz broke down in tears again.

"'Take your underwear off, Lorenz,' he ordered. I just stood there—my mouth wide open, shaking my head in disbelief. He lunged towards me, grabbing the waistband, but I jolted away and they snapped back on. I turned and I ran, as fast as I could. Once I was far enough away, I put my shorts and shirt on again and snuck back into the college, going back to my bedroom, barricading the door with that bed and sitting up all night waiting for the possibility of Cole turning up. I don't know what happened after I left. I didn't dare look back.

"You didn't tell anyone when it happened?" asked Jack.

"No. I guess I was too embarrassed, and scared. I thought about it, honestly I did. But it weighed on my mind all day so I decided just a couple of hours ago to tell Fr. Culpa, who was going to go call the police straight away and have them take Cole."

I wish here that I could tell you that the police arrived and arrested Cole and that they all lived happily ever after. But unfortunately, I cannot tell a lie. Because who should enter the door at that moment but Peter, looking furious. He rushed up to Lorenz and grabbed him by the collar, but Jack pushed him away.

"How could you?" Peter yelled. "Cole told me everything. You're sick, you know that?" He turned to Jack, "Lorenz killed him and he told Cole the plan before he did it. I checked with James Copperfield as well, Lorenz woke Tom up and they left his room together.

"Peter, calm down. Think about it logically. Lorenz wouldn't do that. Cole's lying."

"Don't tell me to calm down, jerk!" Peter yelled, pushing Jack off him.

He had the same manic look in his eyes that Cole had had in the forest. He was out for vengeance. By this point, Lorenz had backed against the window, his eyes full of horror and fear at the unstoppable anger he saw in Peter.

It was all over in a matter of only a few seconds. Peter charged towards Lorenz, trying to tackle him down so that he could get a square fist to his face. But instead, the window behind them broke under the force of two bodies being thrust towards it, and they fell down in a tangle of arms and legs. I cannot describe the sickening thud of them hitting the ground, nor the feeling of Jack's stomach dropping. From the window high above, Jack could see Lorenz standing up, gripping his arm and wincing in pain. But Peter remained lying on the grass, silent and lifeless.

CHAPTER XIII

"In Him was life, and the life was the Light of men. The Light shines in the darkness, and the darkness did not comprehend it."

—*John 1:4-5*

People may wonder why I have decided to write this whole saga down or from what sources all my information hails from. The events of those harrowing months were soon obscured by other newsworthy happenings, and St. Benedict's slowly faded out of the spotlight of local scrutiny. The story, like all stories, eventually became an "oh yes, I think remember that," and a "what year was that then?" among the locals, so much so that the local town was at risk of losing the true story of what had actually transpired.

To this curiosity, I will answer them. My name is Jack Lapin, and when I was a fifteen-year-old boy, I saw first-hand how horrendously disgusting people can be.

The days following Peter's tumble out of the window with Lorenz went by in a blur, so much so that I think my subconscious has actually tricked my mind into blocking it out. Peter survived the fall, but never recovered. He suffered a debilitating neck injury and was made a quadriplegic, never able to use his arms or legs again. He's still alive, but incapacitated. He struggled physically and mentally for a few years after the accident, I guess you never really get used to something like that. He never married or had kids, but he does find joy in sitting in his wheelchair on his porch staring out across the fields, especially at sunset. He recently took up poetry, he has a lady come in twice a week who he dictates to and she writes it down for him. His poems are actually very good. Like all of us, he has some good days and some not so good. He never returned to school or worked when he came of age—after all, what could he do? The mental stress is the worst for him, the idea of what he could have become had his life progressed unhindered.

Lorenz visits him almost every evening on the way home from work. He picks him up for church every Sunday morning with the du Sabre clan and they all go out to lunch after. As I mentioned before, Lorenz began to change the night Tom died. After the accident with Peter, he became a changed man. Years later, he got married to a nice girl named Grace and had two handsome sons and a beautiful daughter. I sometimes tag along with them for lunch and get to see the fuss of the young du Sabres arguing over who gets to sit next to "uncle Peter" each week. I asked him once what caused him to change his ways, whether he had found God in the darkness and despair of that time. His answer was that he hadn't found God, but that God had found him and dragged him along kicking and screaming. After all, God wasn't the one who had been lost.

They're a wonderful little family. Lorenz and Grace are madly in love and their children are happy and healthy. The boys remind me so much of their father when he was in school, except they're much nicer. They inherited his chiselled jawline and bright eyes. And their young daughter, Épée, has Charmaine's eyes and sandy hair, as well as a lot of wry wit just like her aunt. Lorenz became an advocate for the rights of people with disabilities. He was extremely successful in his studies, earning a masters degree and a PhD, but in the end gave up all of that to create a charity, The Steerforth Society, a clever play on words about steering the lives of children forth in the world. He lives a humble life with his wife and children, enthusiastically tackling anything he feels needs mending. You'll often see him volunteering down at the op-shop on Saturday afternoons with his family, or find him running a game of bingo down at the old folks home on a Friday night. He never sees a need that he doesn't try and fulfil nor a yearning that he doesn't try to satisfy.

There was never enough evidence to convict Cole of anything, and the eventual verdict was that Tom had tied the dumbbell to his own foot. From the moment Lorenz left Cole with Tom on that night, nothing could be proven, even the autopsy found nothing suspicious except for pool water. The final verdict was that Lorenz was telling the truth, but that after Lorenz left, Cole left Tom alone shortly after. I doubt we'll ever know what really happened that night. Cole was moved to a special school to reform him and was made to do community service, but only for a short while before his life intersected back into normal society.

I don't talk to Cole or Charmaine now; I have no reason to. Lorenz tells me they got married and had a girl they named Raven. To all intents and purposes, they lived happily ever after. Raven's grandfather, Lance, dotes on her and supports the family. He found Cole a prestigious job managing the main power plant in the city—he's in charge of many people and makes a good wage. They have everything they ever wanted.

Lorenz stays in contact with them, trying to persuade them to change their ways. They don't approve. I actually bumped into Cole the other day while walking along the street. I tried to avoid him but he recognised me in a heartbeat and made his way across the street to heartily shake my hand. I was not as zealous. He told me about his life, how everything had been going well. He told me he had heard about Peter's circumstances and that it was a shame.

"I don't understand why Lorenz spends so much time on him," he complained. "If you can't help them all, what's the point in helping any of them?"

"What do you mean?" I asked innocently.

"Well, you know, it's not as if he can solve all the problems that every downtrodden person has. Why bother helping any of them? If you can't fix a problem, there's no point trying. And he has three kids to look after, you'd think he would be prioritising them with what little money he has. I don't know what his problem is."

"What his problem is? Well I don't know exactly what you mean but I'd say it's fairly obvious you have something to do with it. He still thinks about Tom's death a lot, and about Peter, if that event is even something you'll indulge to remember."

"Now look here," he was starting to get defensive, "if you think I haven't had my fair share of suffering during the years between then and now, well I have. Life has been hard on me too. And we can't all just flip a switch and pretend we've become better people. In some ways I wish I had taken the fall out the window – wouldn't have to go to work every day, that's for sure."

"Well, anyway, I best be off...nice seeing you again Cole," I lied.

"No problem. Nice seeing you too, Joe."

"Jack," I whispered inaudibly as he walked away.

There was no point discussing it with him. I could tell that, to him, he had done nothing wrong, that things had just worked out the way that they had and that they had worked out well for him. So I bid him adieu and continued on my way. I assume that at some point, whatever has been holding him and Charmaine together all this time—their huge excess of money, their over-enthusiastic sex drive, or perhaps simply their nonchalance for the outside world—won't be enough and that their marriage will collapse. Although, saying that, I don't hate Cole. Far from it in fact. I don't think I'll ever understand him or Charmaine as human beings, but I can't hate them. They're just being themselves.

Lorenz, on the other hand, still tries to sway them. He doesn't see them as much as he would like to, but they're now the only family he has. He was completely disowned by Lance when he refused the call to the military life. He still sends a Christmas card each year to his dad. I actually had the pleasure of reading last year's card before he sent it, here it is translated from his scrawling French handwriting:

> *Dear Father,*
>
> *Joyeaux Noel and happiest of greetings to you. We do hope to hear from you soon; the children would love to meet their grandfather whom I know they would love very much. We are happy and healthy.*
>
> *With much love and prayers for you from my part of the du Sabre family: Lorenz, Grace, Felix, Épée, and Thomas.*

As for everybody else involved in these events? Well, they went their separate ways. Charles Latan was fired in disgrace after the inquest. Mrs. Culpa also decided to step down from her position and the school continued on without them. Father Culpa died last year after a short but aggressive battle with cancer. Peter and I went to his funeral, along with Lorenz's family. The Blacks were nowhere to be seen. It was a beautiful service, hearing about all the lives that he had touched through his short but meaningful existence on this earth. Lorenz, who had become good friends with Fr Culpa after his time at school, read a letter as the eulogy. After the funeral, we had tea and biscuits back at his place and I managed to get a copy of the letter. It had been given to him by Fr Culpa the day after he tumbled out the window with Peter.

Dear Lorenz,

I understand that the last couple of days have brought great distress and hurt. It has brought sadness and disillusionment to us all, but perhaps most of all to you. Always know that I am here to talk if you need to, and that my door is always open.

People often ask me to explain my faith. I tell them to look carefully at the world: the way the breeze rustles through the leaves on a cool evening in autumn, or the splash of colours that lights the sky at sunset. Listen to the birds as they each sing their unique song in the morning, or simply be still and contemplate how perfect the world is in its imperfection. Look closely as each uniquely formed but symmetrical snowflake makes its own way in the unforgiving blizzard, and revel in the hope that the first blossom of Spring brings. We don't need to ask God for a sign, he's already given us one and called it the universe.

But remember this: if we are to change the world, rather than just intend to do good, we must sometimes make sacrifices. Think of the apple tree that stands outside the rectory: the bench underneath it was made from one of its brethren, and yet it shelters passer-byes without complaining.

In life, some of us are born to be priests, and some of us are born to be philanthropists. Some of us play sport, and some of us draw pictures. Some of us will be butterfly catchers, and some of us will collect antiques. Some of us are destined to be struck by lightning, and some of us will do nothing particularly noteworthy at all. No matter what our lives turn out to be, know this: it is never too late nor too early to be the person you want to be. Never.

I hope that you will have the courage to believe in the sun even when it's not shining, the bravery to believe in love even when you're not feeling it, and the faith to believe in God even when He appears to be silent. But most of all, I hope, if you are ever unhappy with the person you've become, that you will have the power to start again and to become who you want to be.

There is a reason why love is represented as a flame. Even a single hair casts a shadow, but a flame has no shadow at all.

Fr. Culpa

Perhaps upon reading this book, someone will ask why I wrote it. I guess this will be my answer: my name is Jack Lapin and when I was a fifteen-year-old boy, I met a greedy, selfish, nasty little kid. But through a happy fault, a *felix culpa*, he became a shining beacon of the purest light. He wasn't the light, but merely a reflection of it, just as the moonlight is merely a reflection of the sun. He was the kindest, smartest, most tenacious person you'd ever meet. He could sort out his life by six a.m., and then go about his day solving all the world's problems, one small act of kindness at a time. He could run and not grow tired, walk and not be faint. He could soar on wings like an eagle. And us mere mortals who trod beside him on his journey? Well, we never felt as if we were walking among birds, we felt like we were flying right by their side with them.